SIXGUN VENUS

Sam Hawkins' wagon train was nothing to get worked up about, and the girls travelling on it — under sponsorship of the Western Marriage Agency — suited it. Except Ellen Copperstone, who soon proved she could handle a gun and had the courage to match her looks. But her gifts did not save her from the kidnapper who struck. Hawkins realized that she must possess something — besides her body — that others wanted. He made up his mind that they were not going to get it.

Books by Cole Rickard
in the Linford Western Library:

RIDERS OF THE WHITE HELL

COLE RICKARD

SIXGUN VENUS

Complete and Unabridged

LINFORD
Leicester

First published in Great Britain in 1996 by
Robert Hale Limited
London

First Linford Edition
published 1998
by arrangement with
Robert Hale Limited
London

British Library CIP Data

Rickard, Cole, *1928* –
    Sixgun Venus.—Large print ed.—
    Linford western library
    1. Western stories
    2. Large type books
    I. Title
    823.9'14 [F]

    ISBN 0–7089–5204–6

Published by
F. A. Thorpe (Publishing) Ltd.
Anstey, Leicestershire

Set by Words & Graphics Ltd.
Anstey, Leicestershire
Printed and bound in Great Britain by
T. J. International Ltd., Padstow, Cornwall

This book is printed on acid-free paper

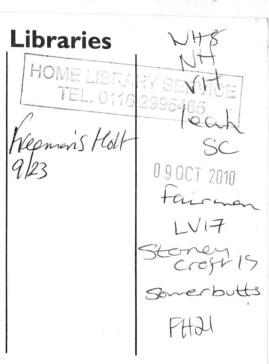

1

SAM HAWKINS rose to his feet. He could not ignore that stifled female cry which he had heard a moment or two ago from the waggon standing closest to the campfire at which he had been sitting. He had been on the edge since the sun had gone down, for he had sensed that Alec Ford had 'something' on his mind and that that something concerned Ellen Copperstone. Ford was a hard man — as tough as they came indeed — and he was used to simply taking what he wanted and to the devil with those who disapproved. Hawkins was only too aware that Ford had lusted after Ellen Copperstone ever since the first moment that he had set eyes on her back in Council Bluffs, and that only the presence of so many people around him had kept the man's hands off her this long.

Hawkins looked down at the remains of his evening meal — and then at the three other cooking fires within the circle of seven Connestoga waggons which he, Ford, Ray Mostegg and Joe Sinclair, were being paid by the Western Marriage Agency of St Louis to guide and protect over the wild and dangerous length of the Oregon/California Trail. He didn't like this, but it had to be done. He was pretty sure that he had glimpsed Alec Ford sneaking into the vehicle adjacent about five minutes ago, and he knew that the other girls who shared that particular waggon with Ellen were 'visiting' on the other side of the camp and having a grand time with their gossip and the bottle of gin that he had so often forbidden. Altogether, though, he supposed he didn't really care what any of those girls were — or had been — and they could go to hell as they wished; which went for Ellen Copperstone too; but the chief travel rule of the Agency must not be broken. The three dozen girls here, being transported in the Agency's name were to arrive in California — at Priceless Gulch, Sacramento, to be precise — inviolate, at least in terms of the Agency's stewardship; because too often girls supplied to prospective husbands in the past had reached their destinations in what was known as 'a delicate condition', and even the roughest miners and logging gentry didn't want to enter the married state with some lusty scout's child coming along. Unhappily, the Agency didn't get paid for the considerable services that it had rendered in the circumstances mentioned, and the Agency, quite naturally, didn't like that. So, if it were a spot of rape that Alec Ford was attempting, a stop would have to be put to it before Ford could sow his wild oats and put Ellen Copperstone's future at risk.

Eight strides carried Hawkins to the rear of the Connestoga from which the choked-off cry had issued. There were wooden steps standing under the tailgate. He climbed these while undoing the ropes that held the canvas door above together with his right hand. Then, the ties falling loose, he parted the flaps at the vehicle's back and peered into the living space beyond, stiffening at what he saw, for Alec Ford, fingers clamped over Ellen Copperstone's mouth, had torn off her petticoat with his free hand and was now tugging at the seat of her drawers. It was plain that, within a minute from now, the piece of sexual violence envisaged would have passed the point of no return; for, regardless of the girl's absolute dissent, she was being easily overborne by Alec Ford's weight and power and could do little to avoid what was being forced upon her.

Heaving himself up level with the entrance, Hawkins swung his left leg over the tailgate and entered the waggon, bowing his head to avoid the brightly burning lantern which had been suspended above the middle of the

Connestoga's floor. "All right, Alec," he said firmly, but without any real threat in his voice — since he was praying that he would be able to put a stop to this without any serious trouble — "give over, mister. She's spoken for at the other end. Some guy in Priceless Gulch has agreed to pay the piper. He called the tune, and we've agreed with the Agency to make sure it's played."

Ford's face had just twisted across his right shoulder. There was murder written on his tigerish features, and his mouth gaped in a dripping snarl. He went for his gun; but Hawkins had been prepared for such a move, and he had jerked and levelled his own pistol before the other man could so much as clear leather. "Don't be a clown, Alec!" he warned. "I haven't shot a man since the war ended, and I don't want this to be the night when I break my cast. Button your trousers, mister, and get out of here!"

"Who the hell do you think you're giving orders, Hawkins?" Ford demanded, releasing the woman whom he had been so near raping and turning to face the covering revolver, his hands moving to do up the front of his pants as had been suggested. "You're getting above yourself, you long bastard! You're only nominally in charge. There's no real boss among us four guys!"

"Unless it be Sam Colt," Hawkins acknowledged, lowering the hammer of his gun and deliberately putting the weapon away. "I'm a man too, Alec, and she's beautiful. I never saw a lovelier girl. But that's it! We've undertaken a job, and we have to do it right. Matter of honour."

"To heck with your honour!" Ford spat contemptuously. "The job will get done right. Our girls will get to California, sure as fate, and without a mark on their lovely hides. It's a long trail, man! What's wrong with doing what comes naturally? Do you figure they don't want it too?"

"I don't even ask myself, Alec," Hawkins replied woodenly. "We know what's right, and we know what's wrong. So do the women. Didn't old Joshua Soap — who owns the Western Marriage Agency — lay down the law to us about it?"

"What a fuss!" Ford sniffed. "Ellen Copperstone has been up the river and round the bend. With many a guy unless I miss my guess. She ain't been Miss Purity in a dozen years. She knows what it's all about, Hawkins, and how to keep herself out of trouble. She won't take any harm from the pleasure one guy can give her — or even two!"

Hawkins' mouth twisted disgustedly. "Don't measure us all by your own bushel," he cautioned. "I still hold a trust as sacred — and so should you. Besides, we're being paid plenty to keep our hands off these girls."

"War widders, jailbirds, drunks, and old whores!" Ford howled scathingly. "What a precious cargo!"

"Maybe," Hawkins conceded. "But so what? For us, their lives began at Council Bluffs. So far as we're concerned, each one of them is Miss Priceless Gulch the same."

"It's laughable!" Ford declared. "You're the clown!"

"I told you to get out of here," Hawkins said, stepping as far over to the left as he could get and gesturing. "There's the door."

"No man pushes me around and gets away with it, Hawkins!"

"Alec, I haven't pushed you," Hawkins responded quietly. "I have spoken to you as one friend to another. All I've tried to do is remind you — and myself — of our duties. Do you find that untrue?"

Ford lowered his eyes. He began moving towards the exit at the back of the waggon, apparently intending to go in peace; but suddenly his head snapped erect and another awful snarl came to his lean and handsome features. His right fist shot out at the same instant, and the blow struck Hawkins on the point of the chin.

Hawkins staggered, his senses reeling, and he was unable to get his hands up before Ford had hit him on the jaw again. This second blow, a hooking left, spun him into a half turn, and he dropped to his knees and his upper body collapsed over the tailgate. A kicking boot tried to lift him over the board, but, at one hundred and ninety pounds, he was too heavy for that; and, frustrated, his assailant seized him by the scruff of his neck and the seat of his trousers and lifted him bodily before pitching him forward and down out of the waggon's rear. His plunge unbroken, he landed on the front of his skull and felt his spine threaten to snap; then, badly dazed and weakened, his lay there in the grass as Alec Ford sprang over the tailgate and landed wholefooted beside him, shaking the earth.

Feeling the toe of Ford's left riding boot bury itself deeply in the soft tissues at the side of his waist, Hawkins uttered an involuntary groan and clawed at the tussocks in an effort to rise.

"Get up, get up, you ugly son-of-a-bitch!" Ford literally screeched in his ear, feet kicking one against the other.

Mortally incensed now, Hawkins did all in his power to obey, but he no longer had the strength to help himself much at all, and he had barely reached his knees when he fell flat upon his face again. Once more hands descended upon him, and this time he was hauled to his feet. Reacting more or less instinctively, he doubled his fists and clapped them towards Ford's head, his knuckles all but coming together as they skidded over the top of the other's skull. Ford gasped with pain, but wasn't hurt in any real sense and, further enraged more than anything else, he thumped punch after punch into Hawkins' midriff, holding him up until he needed a rest, when he stepped back, panting, and let his victim fall supine. "You're finished, Hawkins!" he gasped triumphantly. "Now I'm going to tromp you to death!"

Hawkins gazed up at the other man through a haze. Ford had got it right; he was indeed finished. He saw his enemy close in, and realized that Ford — a two hundred pound man — was about to jump up and down on his already paralysed body until his ribs were shattered and the life left him as fragments of bone pierced his lungs and heart. The prospect, in so far as he still had the wit and feeling to contemplate it, was terrifying, but he knew he'd just have to lie there and let it happen; so he shut his eyes and opened his hands in surrender to the inevitable.

But the worst didn't happen. Instead the roar of a pistol filled the night. Hawkins heard Ford give a yelp of pain and, opening his eyes again, was in time to see his enemy staggering backwards, clutching at his left ear with a hand out of which blood spilled darkly and dripped to the ground. "You hellcat!" Ford yelled now, gazing towards the tailgate of the Connestoga adjacent. "I'll cut your — !"

"That you will not!" declared a female voice in the sharpest of tones. "You will stay exactly where you are!"

Hawkins shifted his eyes to the back of the waggon from which he had been cast down. He saw Ellen Copperstone standing behind the tailgate. She held a silver-plated Smith and Wesson revolver in her right hand, and blue smoke was still threading out of the weapon's muzzle. The woman was naked from the waist upwards, but she stood as unflinching as she was unashamed, and Hawkins remembered a picture once seen in a book and was amazed; for Ellen Copperstone was the living image of Venus risen from the wine-dark sea, with her hair falling in a mass of black curls upon her shoulders and breast and a beauty in her face and gaze that was all woman yet eternally innocent. There she stood, the ultimate flower of the human race, with death in her hand, and she said: "Don't make me shoot again, Alec Ford. If I have to fire, you won't hear the bang. Lest you suppose otherwise, that ear of yours was no accident!" Grim, for all its oval shape and perfect features, Miss Copperstone's face turned briefly towards Hawkins. "Are you all right, Sam?"

"I reckon so, Miss Copperstone," Hawkins answered a mite wheezily, though he was recovering already from the numerous blows that he had taken and felt confident that he would live. With a considerable effort, he sat up — because he knew that he had a duty here — and he slipped out his six-shooter once more, covering Ford with it and thumbing back the hammer in the most deliberate fashion possible. "Ford," he went on, "I gave you your chance to behave. Now Sam Colt is in charge. Take your horse and go. Ride back east. And don't ever let me clap eyes on you again!"

"Okay," Ford said, his fight gone and obviously in some pain with his deeply notched ear. "It's Sam Colt I'm listening to, not Sam Hawkins. You I'd never mind. What a sorry mess!"

Hawkins let it go. This time he had done it as between friends. Should there be a next time, it would be done according to Ford's own rules. His eyes probably said as much.

Ford seemed to understand. Nodding, he looked the half naked Ellen up and down, showing an angrily amused contempt, then faced round and moved away. He walked to the eastern semi-arc of the waggons — where the horses belonging to the men were picketed — and shortly after that receding hoofbeats told of his departure into the southwestern corner of Wyoming which the waggon train had been crossing for the last two days. Then, as Hawkins judged that Ford was probably heading for Rock Springs and South Pass, a movement at the tailgate of the waggon adjacent drew his attention to the fact that Miss Copperstone was still standing there in the buff, though now she pulled a corner of canvas over her bare flesh and said: "Thank you, Sam. You know what for."

"If there's any debt, Ellen," he replied, "it's mine. That hellion meant to smash me up."

"Be done by as you did, eh?"

"Now where did I hear about that?" Hawkins wondered.

"A place you haven't been in many a year, I'll wager," the woman commented. "I'm going back inside, and I don't want to see another man in the vicinity of this waggon tonight. If I do, I'll shoot him dead. That goes for you, Sam Hawkins, as surely as it does for Raymond Mostegg and Joe Sinclair. So pass the word and do it clearly!"

"Why — you bet," Hawkins agreed hastily, for this utterly implacable fierceness in a woman previously so gentle and withdrawing was downright disconcerting. Hell, the female up there brought a shiver to his backbone! "Well, then — I bid you goodnight."

"Goodnight," the woman answered, bringing down the two halves of the

15

canvas door at the waggon's back like stage curtains and hiding her magnificent nakedness with almost dramatic effect.

Hawkins eased himself erect. He tested his balance, then walked in a slow and shaky circle, conscious suddenly that the shot fired from Ellen Copperstone's pistol had brought out all the members of the waggon train from their vehicles and down onto the inner circle of grass where the campfires burned. He felt eyes upon him, and heard muttering from among the women closest to him. Pausing then, he gazed deeply into the shadows at the edges of the ring's patchy firelight — wondering where his colleagues, Mostegg and Sinclair, had been located during the trouble that had involved Ford and himself — and then, hearing male footfalls at his back, he craned and saw the two men walking up to join him. "Hi," he greeted. "How much of that trouble over Ellen Copperstone did you see and hear? If any, of course."

"Most of it, I guess," the gangling Sinclair responded, a frown gathering on the narrow brow above his frank brown eyes. "You didn't handle it right, Sam. Josh Soap did put you in charge, y'know."

"I know," Hawkins admitted. "First off, I didn't want to put up Alec Ford's back higher than it already was. Alec hates bosses. I'm not that struck on them myself if it comes to that. I tried to humour the guy, Joe, and — yeah — it was a mistake. I should have kicked him out right straight off. He knew the rules concerning the women and should have stuck by them."

"You can't humour the Alec Fords of this world, Sam," Ray Mostegg said bluntly. "You're weak, pal. If the guy who pays the wages makes you boss, he's paying you to look after his interest right on through. Ain't that right? You should have fired Alec Ford the instant you found him monkeyin' around in Ellen Copperstone's waggon. He was always going to try it on with that gal some time."

"I'm afraid you're right, Ray," Hawkins said. "As to my weakness, I'd take another look if I were you. Wouldn't you say I usually get done what I want?"

"Okay — okay," Mostegg soothed. "No need to get your dander up. Me and Joe don't mind taking orders from you, Sam."

"Saves the need to think," Sinclair observed cheerfully. "So I neither worry my fat nor lose any sleep."

"You don't get black eyes and split lips either," Hawkins commented wryly. "Alec Ford has the hardest pair of fists I've ever run up against. I'll swear that son-of-a-gun was winding up to put me under the sod."

"No, it wouldn't have come to that," Mostegg said. "Me and Joe were all set to step in when Ellen Copperstone appeared with that gun of hers. We thought we'd leave it to see how she made out." He chuckled. "She did real good, Sam. Fancy her keeping a hogleg up her skirt!"

"Fancy her being able to shoot like that!" Sinclair echoed. "Wonder where she learned? You ask yourself about these gals when you see what we saw."

"She's Venus with a sixgun all right," Hawkins growled. "But don't start getting curious about the rest of it. We don't need to know. Leave the lady to her privacy. We're short-handed now, boys, so we don't want anybody getting shot. If Ellen Copperstone asks for help, help her. Otherwise — walk wide."

"They're all bags of mystery!" Mostegg affirmed, a strong figure of no better than middle height who had a habit of reaching up with his head, as if to equal the lanky Sinclair's six-feet one inch and the similar height of the far more heavily built Hawkins, whom he now shook playfully by the arm. "They've declared to a girl they want to bring comfort and joy into the lives of lonely men, but we know they're all dead set on ending up Mrs Pots-of-Gold!"

"I couldn't wish 'em more success!" Hawkins declared, feeling gingerly around his bruised ribs. "The sooner we get them to Sacramento and draw our pay from the bank, the better I'll like it." He drew a slow and careful breath. "Boys, I hurt. It's me for the sack."

"Not before we've cleaned you up some!" Mostegg protested, his big nose and cleft chin thrusting. "You ain't fit for them women to look at!"

"Never was," Hawkins sighed, making for the spot where he had earlier dumped his bedroll. "If you must clean me up, you'll have to do it in the morning. Tomorrow's just got to start better than today's ended."

But it occurred to him in the same moment that it was always unwise to tempt fate.

2

PERHAPS because of the pangs of suffering which infiltrated Hawkins' consciousness at intervals during the night, it felt as if he had been asleep for no more than an hour or so when a hand came heavily to rest upon his shoulder and shook him hard, robbing him immediately of what peace and comfort his bed upon the earth still held for him. "What the Sam Hill!" he croaked angrily, turning his head on the saddle that he was using for a pillow and rolling a bleary eye upwards at the shadowy figure bending over him in the morning light. "What's going on?"

"Get up, Sam!" Ray Mostegg's voice urged, the panting undertone present enough in itself to suggest a crisis. "Don't just lie there, man! We've got some real trouble now!"

"Real trouble?" Hawkins mouthed

thickly, sitting up abruptly almost at once and paying for it as daggers of pain plunged through his brain. "What d'you mean?"

"It's Ellen Copperstone again!"

"What about Ellen Copperstone?"

"She's gone."

"Gone!" Hawkins kicked back his blankets. "Where's she gone?"

"That's it — if only we knew."

Hawkins forced himself to think coherently, while his skull went on throbbing. "She ran away during the night?"

"Ran away, no!" Mostegg responded in exasperation. "It seems she went for a wash, Sam, about three-quarters of an hour ago — at that little stream yonder we've been getting our water from. You know her habits. That one's a cleanly creature, and she kind of likes to attend to her ablutions ahead of everybody else, when she can. This morning she could, and she did. The other girls in her waggon took no more notice than usual when she got up before them. Like that ginger pussy, Sadie Hulme, said to me: Ellen's a law unto herself anyhow, and in the end she will always do what the hell she pleases. But even they wondered when, a half an hour later, she hadn't come back; so they went over to the stream — in their time — and there she was gone."

"Hot damn!" Hawkins exploded, jacking himself erect, his aches and pains receding into nothing as consternation took him over. "There are grizzlies about, and lions too. Like as not, Ray, that girl's breakfast!"

"It was neither bear nor cougar," Mostegg contradicted. "Her towel and soap and brush and comb was lyin' neat as you please beside the water. Her stockings too. There ain't no ifs and buts, Sam; she was plain and simple grabbed!"

"Taken away? By somebody? Who?"

"Who d'you think?"

Blinking, Hawkins felt oddly surprised by the name which came to him at once. "Alec Ford?"

"Sure, Alec. Figures, don't it?"

"I suppose it does," Hawkins admitted, realizing that he had been thrown by imagining that the man in question had been sobered by what had occurred last night and now ridden many a mile from here.

"Well?"

Hawkins picked up his gunbelt from where it had fallen when he had unlatched it before getting into his blankets the night previously. Now, swinging the belt around his middle, he buckled it up again, easing everything into its correct place and then tying the holster down to his right thigh. "What?"

"Well?" Mostegg repeated waspishly. "What d'you aim to do, boy?"

"Go over to the stream," Hawkins said, shrugging. "Have a look-see. What else? You don't expect me to bound onto my horse and go flying, do you? Hell, Ray! A fellow's got to get some notion of what he's about. Two spits and hope for the best won't do. This is real serious! I've always had Ellen Copperstone down for a 'somebody', and there could be somebody back East to kick up a real stink if she's vanished." He sighed, ramming fist and palm together. "Oh, come on! What's the good quarrelling about it? Let's get over there!"

Leaving the circle of waggons, they walked quickly across the hundred yards of tussocky meadowland to the south of the campsite and came to the nearer bank of the wide, free-flowing stream which Hawkins had seen at the end of the day before as a first rate source of fresh water and perhaps fishing too — for it never hurt to vary the diet when the opportunity arose, and everybody preferred a newly caught trout to salty old stockfish — but right now niceties of that kind were far from his thoughts and his stomach was still churning from the shock of being awakened so abruptly. On top of that, he did indeed fear that this Ellen Copperstone business could blow up into something big. For not only was Miss Copperstone the outstanding girl in the party of females for whom he was responsible here — and probably of good family to boot — but, if it did all end in major crime, like rape and murder, he and his friends could find themselves in court and victims of the kind of scathing criticism which followed men for the rest of their lives and put further well-paid and responsible work beyond them. Reputation was everything, and the West was particularly hard on men who fell into disrepute through any kind of failure in their dealings with women. Too often, as the years confused memories, the innocent were lumped together with the guilty and blamed alike, and this was just such a case where that could happen. Hawkins pulled himself together with the hardest of jerks. He must give what had occurred here everything he'd got. Not only for the sakes of Ellen Copperstone and himself, but those of Ray Mostegg and Joe Sinclair also. Those two guys were able enough in their own sphere — and had long since learned what a cruel varmint their fellow man could be — but of an unending stigma carried into a mindless and vindictive future they had yet to encounter the first thing.

"There's the girl's soap and such," Ray Mostegg said, pointing out the personal items which he had mentioned that Ellen Copperstone had left neatly placed on the bank of the stream. "Ain't no trace of blood or sign of a struggle. I reckon she was just picked up and carried away. Maybe given a knock on the head first. To keep her quiet."

Hawkins nodded mechanically. He could see a number of women from the waggon train moving nearby. They were prowling the water's-edge rather aimlessly. But Joe Sinclair was present too — ferreting at the edges of a thicket of brambles and scrub willow off to the left — and he had an altogether more purposeful air about him. "Found anything, Joe?" Hawkins called.

"This is where the horse stood," Sinclair shouted back. "The critter took a leak and lifted a turf. Couple of cigarette butts too. But nothing that helps any. Just confirms there was somebody here not long ago."

Hawkins suspected that Joe Sinclair was being a sight too modest about his finds, but he said nothing and walked towards the other, Ray Mosteg tagging along. The two men joined Sinclair a few moments later. He led them to the back of the thicket, where he showed them the raised divot and the two cigarette ends which had been stamped out not far from it. Standing over the squashed butts, with his back to the faintly gurgling stream, Hawkins gazed towards the circle of Connestogas, aware that he had a perfect field of vision from this spot while the top of the thicket would almost completely hide his presence from anybody looking in the opposite direction. This would be where Alec Ford, knowing Ellen Copperstone's morning habits, would have taken up his vigil all right. From here, too, while she knelt at the water's-edge, he could easily have crept up on her through the fringe of greenery which followed this northern bank of the flow. There was nothing complicated about any of it; the set up was indeed as simple as could be. The predictable Ellen had clearly walked into Ford's little trap like the nice and unsuspecting girl that she was. "Found any sign leading in or out, Joe?" Hawkins asked. "We can't quite take it for a certainty that our man rode east with the girl on his saddle."

"I'd stake most of what I own on it," Sinclair said. "You can see that broken willow tip on your right. The break points downstream. It's the sort of damage you'd get from a guy fending off the branch with his right arm while holding on to a heavy object with the other."

"Tracking ain't my strong suit," Mostegg observed.

"Nor mine," Hawkins confessed. "That grass is as springy as bubwire, and there's been no rain in a while."

"It's not easy to be sure about much," Sinclair acknowledged, "but something's got to be done."

"It's about to be done," Hawkins said decisively. "Very shortly now I'll be heading for Rock Springs."

"It's a gamble, Sam," Mostegg said.

"How d'you mean?" Hawkins asked uncertainly.

"Should be plain enough," Mostegg answered. "You're speaking of a destination, man. Would a guy with what Ford seemed to be workin' up to be going anywhere in particular?"

"Finally, perhaps," Hawkins growled.

"Once he's had the girl — ?" Sinclair reflected.

"He won't want her any more," Mostegg agreed. "Fellers like him are like that. He'll simply want to be rid of her. He's a mean hand with a knife too.

I can see him cutting the poor girl's throat and throwing her body into a ravine."

"I suppose there's some chance Sam will be able to stop him doing that," Sinclair mused. "Ford's horse is double-burdened. He won't be travelling so fast. Sam'll likely overtake him. Ought to — easy."

"Easy?" Mostegg asked scathingly, casting an eye around the misty ridges and rearing forests of the skylines to the north and east of them. "In this country, Joe?"

Hawkins couldn't stand the shadow of despair which seemed to be descending on everything. "You've got to get a square look at what's there, boys. Ford may have his way with the girl. Chances are, nobody can stop that now. But I can't believe he means to kill her afterwards. He may be a fool where his manhood's concerned, but I've found him canny enough where the rest's involved. Rape and murder are hanging offences and, with the law as organised as it is nowadays, he knows the marshals would ride him down. Remember, we'd all testify against him to the limit we could. There's nothing spur of the moment about any of this. It was all premeditated. Alec had thought it out, and he won't put his life at risk." The speaker nodded emphatically at his own findings, then added: "Sure, I know it all sounds contradictory — when regarded as a whole — but I've got a feeling Alec aims to take Ellen Copperstone to Rock Springs when he's done with her. Even to — somebody. There could be more to this than meets the eye."

"Now you are waxin' fanciful," Mostegg said, more or less dismissively. "That would change the whole complexion of the affair."

"Maybe," Hawkins allowed. "Just trying to make the best sense of it. Because, when you start to think more deeply about it, Ray — and you get the hard facts about Alec Ford's character clear in your sights — the notion that a man of his intelligence would come back here just to seize and rape a woman, when there's so much risk and inconvenience bound up in it, doesn't altogether fit the bill."

"Well, it suits me for reason enough," Mostegg said bluntly. "You're out-smarting yourself, Sam — losin' your grip!"

"Yeah, Sam," Joe Sinclair affirmed censoriously.

Hawkins showed his palms and turned away. He had to admit to himself that his colleagues could be right. His alteration of viewpoint had arisen from spotting the subtleties and playing a sudden hunch. But a guy could get too smart for his own good; and that was a fact. So he put space between himself and his companions, striding fast; and it wasn't until he was thirty yards beyond them that he craned abruptly and called back: "You two get the waggons moving! Sweat some fat off those girls! Yes, we're one short, but there are thirty five others to get to California! don't look for me! Just keep 'em rolling! I'll catch up with the train, as and when. Okay, boys?"

Sinclair bellowed an affirmative, and Mostegg nodded and waved. Now Hawkins accelerated from walking into a run. He swiftly approached the camp which the waggons ringed. Entering it, he went at once to the place where he had slept and rolled and tied his blankets. Then he picked up the saddle which he had used as a pillow and, carrying it and his bed, strode to the corner in which the riding horses were picketed. Here he saddled up and tied his bedroll behind his cantle; and then he led his mount off the campsite through a gap between two waggons and swung up, leaving the circled Connestogas with his rowels digging and his reins on the thresh as he headed eastwards down the line of the waggon road which extended all the way back to Council Bluffs in Iowa.

For all that he rode hard, Hawkins kept his eyes lifting, but his mind inevitably went back to the recent doubts that Mostegg and Sinclair had expressed as to his latest reasoning. He feared for Ellen Copperstone's life much as they did; but human existence was permeated by uncertainty from start to finish. Nothing was done until it had actually happened. He must regard the girl as still alive and in need of his most urgent help until he found her lying dead. If that should be the end of it, he would go on and kill Alec Ford himself. The man might or might not be able to hammer him in a fairly run fistfight, but, when it came to gunwork, Hawkins had seen enough to be sure that Ford was barely in his class. He could outdraw or outshoot the man seven days a week and, short of the other putting a slug in his back, he was convinced that he would win out if it came to a showdown. So look out Alec Ford!

With a dozen miles covered, Hawkins gave a thought to his sweating horse and slowed down, keeping the animal at no more than a fast trot. The land around him was rugged and harsh, a raw and heaving emptiness for the most part — though he knew that in fact there was plenty of life about — and he felt the aching loneliness of it with his mind and body, the inborn sadness of the yawning spaces seeming to increase his misgivings by the mile. On the reasoning that Joe Sinclair had expressed, he ought to have spotted Alec Ford and the girl whom the man was holding captive before now — that was always assuming they had come this way — for a double-burdened horse must be feeling the tests imposed by the country after the present length of travel and be labouring on the climbs at least. Yet while Hawkins knew this explained his uneasiness, it was no less obvious that he was looking at ten thousand hiding places about the waggon road — in fact the Oregon Trail just here — and it was equally worrying that Ford could have taken the woman into any one of these. But there was nothing sure that he could do to resolve any of it, and his underlying helplessness went on tormenting him as it had for a long time now.

On several occasions Hawkins was tempted to turn to one hand or the other in his dilemma — if only for the relief of making a significant change — but he went on riding straight ahead nevertheless, responding to the human attraction of the town of Rock Springs, which could not now be more than twenty miles away; and it was in the late morning, when he had come to within five miles of the place, that he saw a waggon train approaching him at the desultory pace of all such ox-drawn caravans and moved over to his left to let it pass. Then, suddenly inspired to it by the friendly appearance of the large, bearded man riding a sorrel horse out in front of the train — the waggon boss no doubt — he cupped a hand to his mouth and called: "Can you spare a moment?"

The other neither spoke nor made

a sign, but he left the head of his column at once and cantered out to where Hawkins had just reined to a halt. "Can I help you?" he inquired.

"Maybe," Hawkins responded. "Have you passed a fellow and girl by any chance. He sits tall, and she's dark and a real eyeful. They could be riding the one horse."

"Together you mean?" the other queried.

"That's what I mean," Hawkins agreed.

The bearded man paused between a grin and a frown, his face, as seamed and craggy as the surrounding terrain, soon inclining to the latter as he said: "I'm Jake Woodward, of Columbus, Ohio, and may I ask your name?"

"Sam Hawkins, Decatur, Alabama. For what damn good that does here." He smiled wryly. "Unless you believe you may need name and place for the sheriff."

"Doubt it," Woodward said easily. "My business isn't with sheriffs."

"Now mine could be."

"I see," Woodward commented. "No, I haven't seen a couple riding as you describe. But I did pass a couple riding a mile or two back. Heading into Rock Springs, I'd say. He was on a buckskin; she was on a brown pony. I couldn't tell much else about them. They kept well clear, but I could see he was tall and the girl was black-haired."

Hawkins sighed. "I guess the world is full of tall men and girls with black hair at that."

"Not this part of it," Woodward observed, glancing over his shoulder as the waggon train creaked and rumbled westwards to his rear, bullwhips cracking in the flailing hands of the teamsters and voices singing out a monotonous encouragement to the bowing teams of oxen about which dust and flies clouded in the same aggravating fashion. "Have they done something wrong?"

"They don't sound like the right pair," Hawkins said uncertainly. "If they were the right pair — he has; but she's innocent enough. Were they riding close to each other? Did they appear friendly?"

"They were riding close, and they seemed friendly enough. Hard to tell things like that."

"Reckon so," Hawkins admitted. "Well, thanks."

"You're welcome, son," Woodward responded. "That's all?"

"That's all, Mr Woodward," Hawkins acknowledged — "and the best of luck to you!"

"Aye, it's a long way to Portland, Oregon," Woodward agreed, raising a hand in salute and then tugging left, his spurs biting as he galloped back towards the head of the still slowly passing waggon train.

Hunched over his pommel, Hawkins watched the other's progress until he resumed his place at the front of the column; then, stirring up his own horse again, he moved off in the opposite direction once more, at least puzzled by what he had just learned. Life had taught him that no form of coincidence should ever be ignored; and that, even when it seemed in a high degree improbable, events and their elements could and did repeat. Yet two tall young men and two dark-haired girls travelling the back of beyond this morning? The buckskin horse fitted in nicely too. Ford's mount was distinctive: a reddish dun with yellow shadings in the darker colour and a broad streak of grey down its back. But where had the brown horse come from? And how could Ellen Copperstone and Alec Ford even have appeared friendly? Hawkins had once heard the phrase 'natural antipathy' used. He could only guess at what it meant, but he reckoned it might have been coined for that pair. Their hatred of each other had certainly been sprung from hell!

3

THOUGH still gnawed at by the same old uncertainties which had been undermining his peace of mind all the morning, Hawkins nevertheless rode towards Rock Springs in the growing conviction that neither coincidence nor elements of the same had any place here. He was confident that it had been Ellen Copperstone and Alec Ford whom Jake Woodward had passed a while ago. There must indeed have been some kind of link between the pair — if only through the influence of a third party somewhere — about which he had been uninformed and suspected nothing before today.

After all, as he had intimated to Ray Mostegg and Joe Sinclair last night, it was never his policy to pry into the backgrounds and private affairs of the people for whom he made himself responsible. Journeying back and forth across the continent — by waggon train or anyhow else — was an exhausting business, and it left little time or energy for other things. He found it much wiser to remain ignorant for earlier histories of folk with whom he had a travel connection and to let them go on as they were today. It made for the smoother running of things. Anyway, you had to accept that people were good at hiding matters which they did not want others to know about. There was nothing you could do about that, and clever persons like Alec Ford and Ellen Copperstone would naturally be better at it than most.

Hawkins' new belief concerning Ford and the girl forced him to consider those earlier vague thought patterns of his again. For while he believed that Alec Ford was capable of committing rape and murder, he was close to certain that the man was too self-protective to risk his life carrying out capital crimes in circumstances where the witnesses were many and his guilt fairly obvious. Last night he had been plainly in the wrong and correctly sent packing for it. No sound judge would argue it otherwise. Therefore, Ford had returned to the Marriage Agency train earlier that morning only to seize and carry her off to a purpose higher than molesting her sexually. It must figure, then, that if he didn't want her for himself, he had only taken the risk that he had of returning to the train for somebody else. The brown horse suggested that too. A horse was a valuable creature and, even if Alec Ford had had the money to buy one — which was doubtful — where would his market have been for such a quick transaction? He certainly could not have travelled from the waggon train to Rock Springs and back in one night. Aside from the time element involved, it would be almost physically impossible; which meant that somebody not too distant from that train had had that brown horse waiting. And that, taken a step further, meant that the Marriage Agency waggon train had been dogged. Why and for how long? Those were questions which he could not possibly answer here and now, but to which a little nosing around in Rock Springs might just supply solutions. Anyhow, he was duty bound to recover Ellen Copperstone — even if it should turn out that there were reasons why she had not been too unhappy at being abducted by Alec Ford. Or even that, in reality, she had not been abducted at all. For, though there might be little to go on at this stage of the matter, there had to be more to Miss Copperstone than he had ever imagined, and her story could also turn out to be a bigger one than he had dreamed.

Hawkins was still buried in his thoughts — and seeking after some all-important detail that he might have missed — when a tiny missile ripped through his saddlehorn and the bang of a rifle warned him that he had been shot at. Deeply shocked since an attempt on his life was about the last thing that he had been expecting — Hawkins' mind went blank for a second that seemed an age long, and he sat there in the saddle, gaping around him and almost offering a tacit invitation for the bushwhacker to fire on him again. And it was a prompting that was accepted. For the rifle cracked a second time and Hawkins felt the bullet pluck the collar of his shirt, missing about as narrowly as it could miss without doing him some bodily harm, and his mind came abruptly back to life and his responses to it were instantaneous.

Seeming to roll out of his saddle rather than actually spring to the ground, Hawkins came to rest in a crouch on the near side of his horse, jerking his revolver in virtually the same movement. Now, thumbing back his weapon's hammer, he sank still further towards his heels, peering out from beneath his mount's barrel at the scree-littered slope which rose steeply to the south of him.

He could make out gunsmoke curling upwards above a cluster of rocks towards the top of the acclivity, and it seemed to him that the muzzle of a long gun was just visible in the narrow gap between two of the front boulders. With no definite target in view, Hawkins held his fire — waiting hopefully for the other to make a mistake, but expecting no such luck — then, to his surprise and delight, he saw his would-be killer rise out of cover and peer forward and down, clearly seeking some part of his quarry's protected figure to aim at.

Sinking fully onto his left knee, Hawkins tilted his Colt upwards and fired twice — doubting if a hit were possible from the angle at which he was shooting — but his slugs must have travelled pretty close, for the bushwhacker's rifle went flying from his grasp in a fashion that told it had been struck by a bullet and literally torn from his hands. The weapon clattered down well beyond the spot where its owner stood, then slid still further beyond the man's reach, coming to a stop in an area where the watcher below could not actually see it but knew that it was almost outside the bushwhacker's field of recovery. Hawkins expected his enemy to resume the fight with a handgun, but then he realized that the other was not carrying a pistol. The rifleman must either risk attempting to recover his Winchester or take flight over the rimrock without delay, and his hesitation was nearly palpable.

Rising, Hawkins backed away from his mount, aiming his revolver as the angle over which he could point it lengthened and became more favourable to his eye, and he triggered off a close one, hoping that it would persuade the man high above him to take his chance and get while the getting was good; but the bushwhacker, either foolishly brave or unusually stupid, sidled out of his cover and, crouching gingerly, began easing his way downwards over the loose underfoot towards the point some yards below where his rifle lay.

This time Hawkins took even greater care with his aim, and he squeezed off with his sights lined on the brass buckle of the belt that encircled the would-be killer's waist. It should have been a mortal hit, yet Hawkins missed for all his care — but there was no need for another shot, since the man at whom he had just fired lost his balance amidst the sliding stones of a small avalanche that his movements had started above him. In an effort to regain his footing, the threatened man reached high and attempted to dig his heels in, but he literally danced on empty air and then planed outwards, boots to the fore, and crashed down on his back, the carpet of rubble which he had set in motion picking him up and spinning him first on his seat and then lengthwise. After that the dust tended to hide his shape, though his whirling presence became more and more like that of bones passing through a glue factory mill, and he eventually ended up as bloody and shattered limbs sticking out of the thickest part of a fuming comber of debris that spilled away from the foot of the slope and arrested with a roar against a low ridge of fencing granite which bordered the edge of the waggon road adjacent.

Hawkins kept well back. He gave the residue of the avalanche a minute to settle. Then he walked over to the slide and clambered on top of it, unearthing the inert figure of the bushwhacker from where the debris was piled thickest, and he saw that the other was as surely dead as he had feared must be the case. The man had sustained multiple injuries, and those to his spine and skull would have been more than enough to kill him without all the rest.

It was a bloody and unpleasant job, but it had to be done. Hawkins half lifted and half dragged the corpse over to the Oregon Trail. There he straightened the body up and dusted it off. He realized then that the deceased was little more than a kid — not more than twenty-one or-two years old — and that he was an ill-favoured varmint too. Hawkins had never set eyes on the other before in his life, and he was almost certain that the same must have been true the other way round. It made him shiver inwardly to think of a soul so brutal that it could contemplate murdering a fellow man without knowing the first thing about its intended victim and almost certainly for monetary gain alone.

Hawkins had earlier put his gun away. Now he drew it again and stood reloading it while thinking about what he ought to do next. He supposed that he would have to carry the dead man into Rock Springs with him. He could hardly leave the remains of this skinny, bent-nosed, already balding youngster for somebody else to find. Though why not? When all was said and done, the avalanche had killed the bushwhacker and there was no gunshot wound upon him. Yet the retrieval of the corpse from the landslide would probably be

51

traced to him eventually, and that could lead to trouble with the law. Bother of that sort he could do without, since it could lead to a further delay of his now woefully undermanned waggon train in the future. The law and its inquiries could take for ever — especially when some obstinate guy behind a star got the impression that he had been deceived by a smart ass.

Spinning his Colt back into leather, Hawkins gave the leather a somewhat graphic smack. He was back into crisis thinking again. This business was becoming even more of a facer than it had at first threatened. Just who the devil had sent that young polecat out to gun him down? Sure, the kid could have been some inept breed of highway robber, but that explanation of the attempted killing had no ring of truth about it. For he would swear that the rifleman had been hastily hired and instructed in Rock Springs. By Alec Ford? Somebody else? Or, again, by Alec Ford on behalf of somebody else?

If Hawkins had at first had the suspicion that all which had occurred so far amounted to nothing more than a haphazard falling together of basically unrelated events into an apparently ominous pattern that had no larger significance in fact, he no longer had any such foolish notion. The considerable effort that must have gone into the attempt to bushwhack him could only mean that he was regarded as a threat by characters who were for the most part unknown to him as yet. It also certainly looked as if Ellen Copperstone were a major player in some form of perhaps big trouble that had pursued the Western Marriage Agency of St Louis waggon train westwards from Council Bluffs, with Alec Ford always present as its watcher and possibly a good deal more. Well, he, Hawkins, still hadn't the first idea of what it could all be about, but he had to admit to himself that, if he hadn't been so all-fired determined to mind his own business, he would have recognised the special propensities for good and ill in Ellen Copperstone from the beginning.

Apart from her beauty, the girl was obviously an exceptional person in every way. She had education, the social graces, natural poise, and the habits and accent of a member of the upper crust. That she had come from the Old States he was certain, and that she had known far better days he was equally convinced. Yet very little else concerning her added up. For her education and personality alone were more than enough to protect her from any need to marry some roughneck illiterate in a Californian mining town. Though she might be without money today, Hawkins would swear Miss Copperstone could swing the world upside down any time she wished and shake from its pockets the fortune she needed. Short of whim or an unseen compulsion — and he had little belief in either — there could be only one explanation of why Ellen

Copperstone had signed up with the girls seeking their marital fortune in Priceless Gulch, and that was that she had believed the Agency's waggon train a secure hiding place from her enemies. In that, however, she seemed to have been mistaken.

Hawkins reckoned that he had taken his evidential speculations about as far as they would go for now. He needed some new developments to champ on. So, gathering himself for the effort, he turned and again faced the slope off which he had been fired on. Then he went to it and scrambled upwards, experiencing a very strenuous climb to the top, but he made it without accident and crossed the rimrock, gazing down across a stretch of gently falling grassland beyond.

Here, at only a short distance from the brink himself, he came upon a boulder-pile and the horse that was tied beside it. The animal could only be the late rifleman's, and Hawkins freed it and then led it away from the rocks, moving eastwards with the summit and finally down into the shadow of a reverse wall that was crumbling everywhere and matted with moss and ivy. About a hundred yards beyond the end of this bluff — where flat ground extended a long way ahead — he saw the rutted face of the Oregon Trail itself on the left, and he turned on to the waggon road and then led his equine charge westwards along it until they reached the spot where the mount's dead master lay.

Positioning the horse as suited him best, Hawkins picked up the bush-whacker's remains and bent them over the creature's saddle. Then he tied the body in place with his lariat, and after that he stepped astride his own horse and used his left hand to sweep up the other's reins. Now he resumed heading for Rock Springs again, having already made up his mind that he would tell the truth of how he had come by the corpse but omit all reference to the fact that the deceased had tried to shoot him. After all, men died in avalanches every year and the details that he meant to exclude mattered only to himself; for it was a damned sure thing that the person or persons who had despatched the bushwhacker — and might have reason to question his story of the man's end — would not be speaking a word in public concerning their doubts.

Hawkins entered Rock Springs about twenty minutes later. The town was a long established one in a beautiful setting on a tributary of the Green River. It was in fact not unknown to him, for he had touched it a number of times in recent years and had allowed a stopover there of thirty-six hours for the members of his waggon train a couple of days ago, so he knew exactly where the sheriff's office was situated and thus able to tie up the horses and then go in and hand over the body in his charge.

Straightfaced, he told his story to Sheriff Brightwell, explaining how he had heard this avalanche ahead of him — just a mile or two back along the Oregon Trail — and had soon come upon the dead man lying in the rubble which the slide had left along the edge of the way. No, sir. He had no idea what the deceased had been doing on the slope, and he did not have any wish to discover how the dead man had come to his fate. He had done his civic duty, and the sheriff knew it all, and could he go now, please, since he had business of his own that was pressing? The lawman, big and square of face and shoulder, regarded him uncertainly for several moments, then gave a rather slow-witted nod, and Hawkins left his presence with a businesslike briskness that was perhaps the biggest lie of all; for he had no clear idea of where he was headed next. Ellen Copperstone might be a prisoner almost anywhere in Rock Springs — or out of the town for that matter — and he could start searching for her here or there was equal vantage. The single thing about which he could be sure was the high degree of danger which was going to invest whatever amount of interference that he could manage to finally inject into the affairs of the men who were holding her. If he didn't watch it every moment, he knew instinctively that he could end the day as dead as the still unnamed young man whose body he had just left with Sheriff Brightwell. Wincing inwardly, he tried to ignore the thought — wondering how much it would have helped if the lawman had been able to provide the dead man's identity — for it now appeared that the bushwhacker had not been a man of Rock Springs, as Hawkins had imagined, but more likely one of those still shadowy figures who were opposing him. That made Hawkins all the more aware that he could be surrounded by enemies, to all of whom he had been pointed out, while he lacked a clue to any one of them save Ford. Whatever the risks that might be entailed, he must get out of this haze of doubt and uncertainty and into the light of true knowledge as swiftly as he could. He was at a loss all round, and what he needed was a genuine break.

He strode up the main street, glancing around him with a jaundiced eye. He studied folk narrowly, and they seemed to do the same with him. Just then he could discern only what was imperfect about Rock Springs. The surface of the street had the appearance of a black and churned crust of pastry, the boardwalks were sunken almost out of sight in dirt that had once been spring mud, clapboard walls were rotting everywhere, and many of the trade signs that jutted on either hand were hanging loose. The scene was, of course, a miniature of the whole urban West, and he wondered briefly how many people were seeing the details as he saw then — or worse even capable of it — and his frustration was running to disgust, when his break arrived with an abruptness that quite startled him. For Alec Ford walked out of a saloon doorway a few yards ahead of him. Turning left, the man began walking eastwards, and there was that about him which suggested that he was headed somewhere that he regarded as important.

With the shock still quickening his pulses, Hawkins feared that Ford might yet make a sudden turn of the head and spot him; so he stepped sideways into the doorway of a shop on his left and then peered along the face of the plate-glass window that jutted before him, keeping the tall man ahead in sight during every moment — for the built-up area of the town was thinning this far out from the centre and Ford's probable destinations could not be that many — and, as he had rather suspected might prove to be the case, the other turned into the last of the larger buildings on this side of the street and passed from view.

Hawkins emerged from his hiding place and resumed his forward movements. He stalked quickly along the boardwalk, raising his eyes to the legend painted in black above the entrance to the stone building through which Ford had just passed. The words up there identified the pile as being the Forkland hotel, and Hawkins supposed that it could be as good a place as any to hold a female prisoner on a short term basis. Anyhow, he reckoned he'd have to search the building through — without being too obvious about it — and that would plainly entail entering the Forkland from the back and hopefully going to work unseen.

Spotting an alley at the western and nearer end of the hotel, Hawkins backed up a yard or two and stepped sideways again, passing into it, and he found himself in a rather gloomy passage which extended to join a corner of the yard at the establishment's rear. Lightly, but without actual stealth, he moved along the narrows, looking for a door in the wall on his right by which he could attempt to enter the hotel, but the soaring structure remained blank down the whole of its length and forced him to keep advancing until he reached the edge of the back yard which was visible from the street.

Growing more cautious now, he inched a short distance into the space before him and gazed along the wall which formed the hotel's rear. Two doors stood open not far to his right, and he could hear activity in the building behind them. The noise did nothing to encourage his closer approach, and he retreated into line with the corner next to his right shoulder and peered upwards, already aware of the rungs in the vertical box structure which supported the western corner of the wooden balcony which ran across the hotel's back at a height of about twenty feet and served all the glass doors to the rooms on the first floor.

Hawkins studied the ladderlike ascent which ended at the balcony's rail. It appeared an easy climb and had to be the perfect way into the hotel for him. So he mounted the steps and went up them without hesitation, coming to the top of the ascent within moments. Then, clinging to the balcony's cornerpost, he swung his left leg over the balustrade adjacent and brought his other leg up to join it, spinning on his backside after that and finally dropping his feet to the floor boards of the raised platform itself.

Now he straightened his back and, settling his displaced gunbelt with firm hands, gazed along the hotel's rear wall at the level of the glass doors. This was where his real problems could begin, for some of those doors — or even all of them — could be locked and the rooms behind them occupied. Perhaps he had tended to take the task which he had envisaged back on the main street a little too lightly. There were difficulties here all right, and he didn't doubt that others would emerge in due course. But it never paid to dwell upon the details of the challenge.

Catfooting now, he moved to the

first of the glass doors and peered through it. The room behind it was unoccupied, but the lock had been turned and did not yield to pressure. Leaving it, Hawkins sidled up to the next entrance in line and, as previously, gazed through the shadowy oblong of transparency before him and into the space beyond. Here again the room was unoccupied, and a twist at the doorknob brought the same kind of resistance that he had encountered at his first attempt to get in. Sighing his annoyance, Hawkins was tempted to bow his shoulder against the frame of the door and use real force, but he realized that this must create some noise — and could even result in the sounds of actual breakage — so he renewed his patience and shifted position for the third time, arriving outside the middle door of those present and looking deeply through the glass.

It was then that he received another of those little shocks. For Ellen Copperstone was sitting in a wicker armchair not four paces beyond him. The girl was clad in the simple dress of grey wool that she always wore while travelling on her waggon, and she was gazing down at the hands resting in her lap. The expression of her face was blank and hopeless — and Hawkins felt anger welling up inside him at her despair. Ellen Copperstone was a fighter and should never look like that.

Scowling, Hawkins put his fingertips against the door and rattled hard at the glass.

4

THE girl looked up sharply, and Hawkins beckoned urgently, his right forefinger tightly crooked. Ellen Copperstone studied his face with startled eyes, not seeming to recognise him for an instant, but then she lifted herself out of her chair and ran to the glass door before her, a hand twisting at the key which had its hinges whispering faintly, and the girl thrust out her face at him, her lips silently questioning.

"Dammit!" Hawkins exploded softly. "You do want to get out of there, don't you? Hell, you're not on their side, are you?"

"No," she breathed — "no. Of course I'm not!"

"Then stop looking so blasted sorry for yourself, Miss Copperstone, and move your butt!"

"You pig, Sam Hawkins!" she responded.

"Yeah," he agreed, "I know all about me. I should have been drowned at birth."

"No less!" she assured him.

"Come on, girl!" he insisted. "Or we're going to get caught, and I'll get my britches dusted!"

"Come on — where?"

"Back where you come from," he replied. "We can climb down the post at yon corner of this here balcony. It's not difficult!"

"I'm not dressed for it," the girl pointed out. "Don't you care about that?"

Hawkins couldn't believe what he was hearing. She ought to be ready to fly the coop like no girl ever was. Instead she was arguing convention — her modesty, he supposed. He gobbled at her, and was on the brink of being downright impolite, but he knew that would only make matters worse; so he swallowed his gorge and said:

"All right. We'll try to leave through the hotel." He advanced into the room where she stood, his movement forcing her back. "Thunderation! Don't you know the g'damned way?"

"Stop swearing!" Ellen Copperstone reproved, spinning away from him then and darting for the door on the right of the room's fireplace. "What foul-mouthed brutes you men are!"

"So don't get me really wound up!" Hawkins warned. "Move, girl — move!"

She ignored his exhortation, stopping dead at the door that she had just reached. Easing the woodwork open, she slowly thrust her head out, looking to left and right. Then she glanced back and whispered: "It's all clear."

He nodded, and she slipped out of the room. Following her, he shoved gently at her shoulder-blades, seeing that they had entered a corridor which appeared to cross the building from side to side. Now she lunged to the right, and he continued to pursue her, following her again as she turned into a passage which opened on the left and provided an unobstructed route into the front of the hotel, where a rail-enclosed stairhead was visible under a window built from numerous panes of glass. Picking up her hems, the girl ran faster than ever — a touch of hysteria about her flight — and she was less then half way across the building, when a little shriek left her as two big men stepped out of a doorway on the right and blocked her path. Checking as Ellen Copperstone checked, Hawkins saw that one of the pair was Alec Ford, while the other was much older and heavier, with a square, ill-tempered face, deeply seamed and wrinkled around the eyes and mouth, bushy sideburns, and a balding, spike-fringed crown which had about it the pasty look of skin that was seldom uncovered to the sun. This second man uttered a curse at the sight of Miss Copperstone which made Hawkins' mild swearing sound like something heard at a picnic for growing boys. "For Chrissake grab her, Alec!" he bellowed, almost knocking the younger man over as he shot out his arms to do what he had just ordered of the other for himself.

Ducking low, Ellen writhed sinuously away from the hands that tried to settle on her body. Then she spun round, virtually on the spot, and dived back in the direction from which she had come. Hawkins turned in a similar fashion, slamming his back against the wall on his right and drawing himself up as tightly as possible in order to let her pass him cleanly. Then off he went in her tracks once more and they returned to the transverse passage that crossed the base of the present one, cornering to the right yet again and pelting back into the room from which they had set out.

The girl headed now for the glass door and the balcony beyond it — which was precisely what Hawkins was silently willing her to do — and, once out into the air, she sprang for the angle of the raised platform where the box-shaped support from below rose vertically into sight. Seizing the barred structure with her right arm, she threw her left leg over the balustrade that met it horizontally from that side and half-turned neatly on to the support itself, her weight achieving the necessary momentum; then, as her feet met the rungs beneath her, she steadied and began almost literally walking towards the ground at a pace which the following Hawkins realized that he could not possibly match. So he did not try. Instead, on reaching the rail at the balcony's end, he swung himself over it, turning to face the balusters in the process, then launched himself backwards and down, plunging to the ground and hitting it wholefooted a couple of seconds before the girl lost the rhythm of her descent on the last of the rungs that she was climbing down and slipped to land beside him in a kick-up of legs and a splurge of lace underwear. "There!" she protested angrily, looking both mortified and bemused. "I told you!"

"Dammit, girl!" he gulped, rising to his full height and helping her up. "Haven't I seen more already?"

"Oh!" she complained, frowning like a little girl. "You are *the* most — !"

"Save it!" he counselled. "Stir yourself — 'cos you can sure move fast enough when you want!"

He expected her to turn into the length of the alley and make for the street. Again he moved aside to provide her with clear passage. But instead she faced in the opposite direction and ran out into the hotel's back yard, heading for the corner of it to the left-hand rear, where open space was visible beyond the Forkland's outbuildings. Suppressing a further oath, he went after her, throwing up his hands in despair as he did so — for it should have been obvious to Ellen Copperstone that they would be safer from molestation on the main street than dodging around on the lots — but she appeared to have missed the fact that they could be chased to the limit yonder and even fired on without the risk of immediate censure holding their enemies in check.

His thought of gunfire seemed to prompt a response in kind from the rear. A pistol banged high up on the balcony which he and Ellen had recently left in such haste. The bullet chipped a fragment from the heel of the right boot, and he felt a jarring sensation pass up the back of his leg and into the lower spine. Craning, he saw Alec Ford bellied up to the rail at the front edge of the raised platform. The man was aiming at him anew, and he sprang aside instinctively, fearing that the next slug would bring him down; but the older guy — he with the bad-tempered looks — was newly arrived at Ford's elbow, and he knocked up the barrel of the younger man's revolver and spoke a sharp word or two in his ear. Ford twisted his head round angrily at the other, seeming on the brink of an outburst, but he controlled himself with a visible effort; then, nodding, went to the cornerpost which had already served the fugitives and essayed descent, while the older man turned from him and hurried back indoors.

Hawkins looked to the front again. He and the girl already had a worth-while lead, and it would be several moments yet before Ford could give direct chase. At the present rate, they ought to clear the hotel grounds before the tall man had really got started, and that should mean they would be safe from any further shots that Ford might fire. Tucking in his elbows and picking up his knees, Hawkins spurted, intending to overtake his companion and provide the lead — and he did draw level with her left shoulder for a moment — but then she sprinted ahead once more and he couldn't catch up for the second time, try as he would, so again he let her go.

Reaching the outbuildings, they passed the end wall of the brick-built stables and came to the boundary fence. The girl stopped, hitching still harder at her already lifted hems to further neutralise the hobbling effect of her dress's close-fitting skirt, but Hawkins saw the pause as unnecessary, and he lifted her off her feet as if she were no heavier than a pennyweight and swung her over the top of the fence, setting her down cleanly on the other side. Then he vaulted over the five bars himself and came to rest beside her, legging it back into motion as she did the same, and they went to the left — where the lot space which extended to ridged earth about a hundred yards to the north of them seemed to narrow in upon the wider settings of the town's larger properties — and, glancing back and seeing that they were as yet unaccompanied on this new stage of their flight, Hawkins reckoned that they should make it to where he had left his mount tied near the sheriff's office without coming under extra pressure. But what would happen after that he was by no means sure; for a double-mounted horse — already tired from a long journey — was not going to achieve much against the fresh animals that could soon be pursuing it. Yes, Ellen Copperstone and he could claim the law's protection and stay here in town — and he would be happy enough to do that if he were certain that his companion was in no sense compromised — but he was far from sure that this was the case. He would only be able to express his final opinion on that one when he knew the precise reason why Ellen had been abducted that morning; for the entirely innocent seldom fell victim to the kind of seizure that had compelled his ride into Rock Springs. He had a nasty feeling that Miss Copperstone was guilty of something, but not the first idea of what. For now he simply prayed that they would stay free long enough for him to ask and find out.

They soon ran on to the ground which paralleled the buildings at the western end of the main street. Now Hawkins judged that it would bring them out close to the sheriff's office if they turned into the third of the alleys that he could see running through the line of properties on his left hand. He began panting out instructions to his companion; but she, with the seeming perversity that he was almost coming to expect of her now, swung aside at the first of the openings and plunged into it, causing him to grind his teeth in outright fury. He had thoughts of catching up with her and kicking her backside, but it suddenly occurred to him that she had the general demeanour of a woman who knew where she was going and had done from the first. "Do you know — somebody in Rock Springs?" he gasped.

"Yes," she breathed just audibly; and a jerk of her head confirmed the reply.

"Well, dammit!" he exclaimed, angrily

amazed. "You are surely a bundle of surprises!"

That was really the end of it then. They were half way down the alley now, and the ringing of their footfalls more or less excluded further gasped words. When seconds later they emerged on the main street itself, he went on keeping silent and let her indicate where they were headed next, and she pointed directly across the way to a passage there that could almost be regarded as a continuation of the one they had just left; and they sped into it with barely a glance to either side and raced to its end, bearing left once more and down a fenced path that issued into the back yard of one of the biggest properties on this southern side of the street. Without checking to even catch her breath, Ellen Copperstone went at once to the rear entrance of the dwelling adjacent and hammered on the woodwork with a clenched fist. "An old friend of the family," she panted across her shoulder by way of explanation.

Hawkins nodded jerkily. When you were baffled by it all, you had to hold your peace and start trusting. He was, for the moment, still worried by the possibility that their line of flight had somehow been traced — at least approximately — to this spot, by Alec Ford, as the main pursuer, or the older man, who could have been watching from higher up the street; but, as the seconds went by, Hawkins' straining ears grew satisfied as to the first part, for no echo of hurried footfalls reached him from near or far, and he began to relax and watch the door on which Miss Copperstone was now beating her knuckles a second time.

On this occasion she received an answer immediately. The door was opened to her by a florid, matronly woman, greying and sad-eyed, who could well have reached the back of the woodwork at the moment that Ellen had repeated her summons. Looking out, the older female drew in her lower lip between yellowing teeth and appeared slightly taken aback. "It's you, Ellen!" she exclaimed. "Where have you sprung from? I imagined you on the Californian Trail by now, my dear!"

"And so I should have been!" the girl responded, in a gasping speech that now owed more to indignation than hard exercise. "Alec Ford — that odious man I told you of the other evening — kidnapped me first thing today and brought me to Rock Springs. It had all been arranged by Horace Lemon, even to the horse I was given to ride!"

"Oh, my dear!" the matronly woman sympathised. "You do seem to be in the wars, don't you? Things have gone horribly wrong for you, haven't they? You had better come in." Looking round Ellen, she fixed Hawkins with an uncertain eye. "Who's the man with you?"

"That's Sam Hawkins, Mrs Kline," the girl answered. "He's by way of being our waggon boss."

"By way of?" the older woman queried, standing aside and gesturing for both Ellen and her companion to enter. "That's a funny way of putting it."

"Oh, it's a dot-and-carry-one outfit," the girl explained rather contemptuously. "That man Joshua Soap of St Louis is meaner than Moses is reputed to have been. His waggons are fit only to be burned, and the brides have to crew them. The old wretch supplied just four men to act as our guides and protectors across some of the wildest country on earth. I ask you, Winifred!"

"It certainly does have a makeshift sound about it," Winifred Kline commented, turning now to lead her callers along a gloomy passage and deeper into the sanctuary of her home, which Hawkins immediately judged to be situated at the back of a shop of some kind that faced onto the street beyond. Now they entered the living room, which was clean and comfortable enough — with thick rugs on the floor, a leather sofa in front of the shingled fireplace, winged armchairs on either side of the hearth, a few good pictures around the walls, and an oaken sideboard covered in the blue of English Wedgwood china — and here Mrs Kline turned and faced them again, brow gathered and palms rubbing together nervously as she asked them to be seated and then added rather apprehensively: "Am I to take it that you're fugitives of some kind?"

"Fugitives of any kind that suits you, ma'am," Hawkins hurried bluntly. "My only interest here is to get Miss Copperstone back to the waggons and on her way to California once more."

"Ellen might not want that now," Mrs Kline said, measuring her words.

"It's what she doggone signed up for," Hawkins snapped — "even contracted to, I might say. There's some guy in California who's going to pay for her ride west and all this damned nonsense."

"He keeps swearing," Ellen said waspishly.

"Swearing, be damned!" Hawkins snorted. "What a precious flower you are, Miss Copperstone! It strikes me as likely my faults pale beside yours. I've the notion you're one hell of a devious young woman!"

"It's hard to like you, Sam Hawkins."

"I'd rather you liked me, Ellen Copperstone, but you're free to do the other thing."

"These are difficult times," the girl said defensively. "You know so little about me. We have to do the best we can when our means are limited and our needs large."

"That includes making mugs of the folk who're prepared to help us, does it?" Hawkins inquired sweetly.

"Aren't they out to help themselves too?" Ellen responded, trying to make her question sound reasonable. "You only see the man's side of it. I don't see it as correct at all that a man should acquire a wife by dint of her misfortunes. Because that's what it adds up to."

"I'm not against you on principle," Hawkins admitted. "But you put it too strongly; it sticks in my craw. Nobody forced you into anything. Somehow I doubt that a Californian marriage ever had a real part in your plans. I have a feeling in my bones that you've been using Josh Soap's Marriage Agency for your own ends. Confound it, Ellen, I'm getting used to being shot at on your account, and that ain't right!"

"Oh, ain't it!" she mocked, standing up to him defiantly. "I'm not going to tell you everything there is to tell just because you keep pumping in that dull-witted way of yours. But this much I will tell you, Sam, just to put you straight. A wedding in California is what I most earnestly seek. Though not marriage to a miner. I have a very different kind of partner in mind."

"She tells of one far more fitted to her birth and breeding," Mrs Kline explained. "Really, Mr Hawkins! I cannot believe that you see this beautiful and accomplished young woman as the wife of some ill-bred lout who digs holes in mountainsides. Pshaw!"

"She's beautiful all right," Hawkins acknowledged, determined not to be too accommodating now that class snobbery had surfaced to the detriment of the working man. "She may be accomplished too; but all I've seen her do is shoot a bit off a man's ear. Now that is one hell of an accomplishment, Mrs Kline! As for the rest, I don't care what she was born. It's what she is today that matters; and that ain't much."

"She's the flower of the Philadelphia aristocracy," the older woman returned, sounding outraged. "The Copperstones were — "

"No, Winifred!" Ellen interrupted gently. "Sam Hawkins is a fair man, whatever else, and his natural intelligence is of a high order. I'll fight with him when he's in the wrong, but there's a lot of right with him here. I'm sure he'll come to a better understanding of me and much else if I just say that it wasn't only Southern families that were ruined by the Civil War. The Confederate soldiery marched through northern lands, early on in the struggle, as Sherman and his men later marched through Georgia. My father and mother were slain, and our estates laid waste. I was a teenage girl — " She broke off abruptly. "But enough of that. Look at Sam Hawkins' face! He thinks I'm trying to play on his sympathies — and, sadly, he could be right."

"Well, it's human enough," Hawkins said shortly, "and a lot of folk have done it one time or another. Why don't we simply stick to the bald facts? What I mean is to get to the heart of this business. Tell me what Horace Lemon wants of you, Ellen. And I'd like to know why you were abducted this morning. If I knew about those two things, I figure the rest would become plain enough without a lot more talk."

"Possibly," the girl said. "Horace Lemon was the husband of my elder sister Mary. She's dead now. Just before the Civil War, at the time of Mary's marriage, my mother gave her — "

Hawkins breathed hard. He was annoyed by the manner in which Ellen had broken off again, yet had noticed the sudden shift in the direction of her gaze and deemed there to be a reason for it. She had heard the same speaker in the front of the building whose voice had impinged upon his own ears. Those finely modulated tones belonged to a young man of good birth and education, and they were ingratiating as they joined with those of an older and gruffer man. The conversation between the pair was very brief and, at this distance, more or less unintelligible, but the lilting tenor overtones of the young man obviously meant a great deal to Ellen Copperstone, for her expression as she concentrated upon them became ecstatic and her eyes actually seemed to glow with joy. Then, all restraint leaving her, the girl ran past to the door and thrust her head into the passage outside it, calling: "Jason! Is that you, Jason?"

"Ellen?" came the equally loud response.

"Through here, darling!" she guided.

Footfalls moved out of the building's front, coming faster and faster towards the living room; and then a very tall young man, blond and of athletic build, swept into the room, bearing the dark girl with him; and they stopped at the middle of the floor and clung to each other, kissing as only lovers could; and when they were finally done with this all too stimulating union of mouths, Ellen broke away from her Greek god and went whirling into a dance step that spun her over to the window, where she halted and looked back into the room. "Let me introduce," she announced with all the joy of a besotted teenager, "Jason Wellard, the love of my life and husband to be! Oh, I'm so happy! No woman could be happier or more grateful to heaven!"

Hawkins pursed his lips and gave his nose a faintly amused twitch. "Hello, Wellard. Nice to meet you. You sure seem to have made an impression on Miss Copperstone."

"Don't I?" Wellard agreed.

Hawkins knew that he should feel happy for the man, but realized that the sudden onset of an inexplicable jealousy was making him feel anything but.

5

RUTHLESSLY purging his mind of an incipient longing — because he believed there was no future in anything else — Hawkins tucked his thumbs into the front of his gunbelt and stood there with his face as straight as could be. He waited for the girl's romantic energies to flare up again and her passionate excesses to repeat themselves — as he was inwardly sure that they must — but then, to his complete surprise, Ellen Copperstone sobered visibly while still gazing at the object of her adoration and bewilderment suddenly appeared in her eyes. "Jason," she then blurted out, clearly unable to maintain the suppressive silence that she would have preferred to keep. "Honey, you're not supposed to be here, are you? You shouldn't be closer to me than

Cheyenne at this time. It was agreed that we see each other again only when I had reached Sacramento."

"Well, yes, dear girl," Wellard said, a trifle mincing and uneasily dismissive — even a hint brazen about it too — "but you know how it is. Needs must and all that, eh?"

"No," Ellen said, a dawning fear seeming to half choke her, "I — I don't know how it is. Explain it to me. Tell me what's happened."

Wellard grinned uncomfortably. His manner became more off-hand than ever — as if he were seeking a form of escape but didn't know how to obtain it — though he appeared to find a kind of relief as the sound of more male voices echoed through from the front of the dwelling. "Who the heck's that?" Hawkins asked tautly, cocking his chin.

"Customers, probably," Winifred Kline responded. "My husband usually sees quite a few in the course of the day. Our store is the meeting place for many. Gold is still being dug along the Wind River mountains — and panned from lots of creeks on the Green river too."

"Adolf Kline, Winifred's husband, is a buyer of gold," Ellen explained, her gaze still fixed on her blond lover. "Well, Jason?"

The young man shook his head. He was wooden to the point of ignoring her. Then the sound of feet approaching from the front of the building was again audible and, exhaling a sigh, Wellard faced about and gathered himself for whatever ordeal he now seemed prepared to admit was threatening. "Ellen," he said gravely, though he was presently showing her his back, "you're not going to like this — and neither am I — but it can't be changed."

"What on earth do you mean?" the girl gasped.

The shadow of a large and ugly figure appeared on the threshold of the room. After that Horace Lemon entered at the door. He held a revolver in his right hand, and the weapon was cocked and threatening. Behind the sour visage of the aptly named Lemon came the devilish but much less repellent features of Alec Ford, while two other tough-looking characters showed dim aspects of themselves in the gloomy background.

"He was wrongly named," Hawkins said ironically. "He should have been called Judas and not Jason. It seems you saw Ellen and me run across the street just now, Wellard. And it also figures that you went along and told Horry Lemon straight off. It's a sure bet for me you've been keeping company with this girl's enemies from the start. While I've still a certain amount to learn, I can see that plain enough. What a spruced up skunk you are for a two-bit college boy!"

"Shut up, you!" Lemon commanded, digging the muzzle of his Smith and Wesson into Hawkins' solar plexus. "Consider yourself our prisoner. You would be dead now if that young idiot

Staines had done his job properly. Disarm the man, Alec!"

Stepping up, Ford plucked the pistol from the captive's holster and thrust it into his own waistband. "You're really up to your neck in it, Sam!" he jeered. "You should have stayed with the waggons. You're outclassed here, mister. It's sure a pity Peter Staines and his rifle didn't finish you though!"

"Is that so?" Hawkins taunted in reply. "There never was a blowfly yet that couldn't blow. Your bushwhacker or you!"

"Haven't you even got the brains to be afraid?" Ford queried, shaking his hand at the prisoner's pretended unconcern. "I hadn't taken you for a complete fool!"

"Nor I you," Hawkins returned. "But I find I was wrong."

"You're as good as dead, Sam!" Ford advised maliciously.

"You've heard the truth, Hawkins," Lemon said shortly. "That goes for my sister-in-law too."

"Horace, you can't mean that!" Ellen cried aghast.

"I can and do," Lemon answered, "and well you know it. We can't have you left around to stir up trouble when this is over."

"Jason!" Ellen begged. "Talk to him, for God's sake! Isn't it enough that you've betrayed a woman who loves you? Do you want her blood on your hands as well?"

Wellard's face was expressionless and his ears apparently stopped. He gazed past the girl and out of the window.

"I can't believe this!" Ellen wailed, appearing utterly taken aback by his reaction to her plight. "Jason, what have you done? I can't believe you told them — "

"He told us everything," Lemon interrupted callously. "Be your age, girl! All about your plan for crossing the country by waggon train and disposing of Mary's jewels with Adolf Kline on the way. It all spilled out of him once we discovered that you and he were involved with each other, and we didn't have to use much persuasion in the matter either. Jason is a handsome boy, Ellen — and I'm sure he gave you some real good tumbles while you were staying with him in that hotel in St Louis — but that's all he's good for. He's no hero, and never to be trusted in anything that matters."

"You can do this to me, Jason," Ellen asked brokenly, "after what we've been to each other?"

"He's had you," Lemon remarked scornfully. "You women take it all too seriously. It's just relief for both parties. He's had you, Ellen, and no longer wants you. Much less needs you."

"How did my sister come to marry an animal like you?" Ellen questioned through her teeth.

"She was looking for the strength her earlier beaux lacked," Lemon explained. "She was a young woman with a remarkable gift for picking weak men. Weak men make good lovers but poor husbands. But the trouble with strong women is that they cannot really tolerate strong men."

"Greedy men," Ellen corrected. "Greedy men — like you!"

"Mary was my wife," Lemon reminded. "Everything she possessed was mine by right. Those jewels of hers were mine — by right of marriage."

"The law doesn't say that," Ellen retorted. "She was free to leave them to whom she pleased, and she gave them to me just before her death. She was well aware that you had already tampered with her will."

"So you fled like a thief?"

"I fled because I knew how you would react, Horace — and didn't you just? The only dishonesty in this is yours!"

"You self-righteous little prig!" Lemon flung back. "Don't talk to me about *your* honesty, my girl. Look where you delivered Mary's jewellery! This is the home of a man who was once among the most notorious jewel fences on the East Coast. Adolf Kline was an expert in breaking up stolen collections and selling off the stones to jewellers elsewhere. He got out of Philadelphia about one jump ahead of the police, and they'd give plenty to know where he is today. Gold buyer indeed!"

"But that's what he is today," Winifred Kline protested, cowering as Lemon swung on her and glowered. "It's an honest trade, sir, and he's an honest man. The volume of our trade in these parts is proof enough of that."

"Fiddlesticks!" the big man contradicted. "The leopard doesn't change its spots, madam. The proof of that is in what your husband had agreed to do for Ellen Copperstone. He was going to break up my wife's fine things: sell off the precious stones — diamonds, emeralds, rubies, sapphires and such — and melt down the gold and silver involved and dispose of it through his junk metal trade. There was to be a nice profit in it for him, and a fortune of some size for Ellen — eventually."

"The Copperstones were our friends!" Mrs Kline excused. "They were good customers and did a lot for us in the old days. My husband was simply trying to repay the past favours of Bart Copperstone by helping his daughter to make a fresh start in life. What with the war deaths of her parents and much else that's been disagreeable, sir, Ellen has been an unfortunate lass. The young deserve a chance."

"Not more than their seniors," Lemon commented, sniffing. "I have had my misfortunes too. Not least of them was in wedding Mary Copperstone. She was an ill-tempered and tight-fisted bitch if ever there was one!"

"She was not!" Ellen declared furiously. "Mary was a sweet woman, and very generous too!" She dashed the back of a hand across lips that were wet with spittle. "Your bad luck has been of your own making, Horace! You've been a dissolute man, and you've gambled fortunes away. Mary realized almost from the beginning that to help you was to throw good money after bad! You were trash before, Horace Lemon, but here you stand revealed as truly evil! If you dissipate the last of the Copperstone fortune in the brothels and gambling houses of New York City, it will be an offence against my sister's memory that I'm convinced God and all the angels will take up. You will be cast down into Hell!"

"Where you can wait on me, you hysterical virago!" Lemon countered disdainfully. "I aim to come up with five times the sum for Mary's jewels that you stood to realize. How does that please you?"

"It may be too late for you," Ellen responded, plainly clutching at straws as her mind twisted and turned in its mounting vindictiveness. "When I gave Adolf Kline the jewels — on my visit here at the stopover of the waggons the other evening — he told me that he intended to act fast."

"Haven't you understood yet?" Lemon

asked in bored tones. "We knew all about everything prior to its happening. Nothing was done. The jewels went nowhere. They are presently locked away in Herr Kline's safe, young woman, and they will soon be lodged in my pocket now. It is done — over. For you it is finished." He paused to grin at her fiendishly. "I may see Sunny California, but you won't. They tell me the gambling on the Barbary Coast is particularly good, and the women the most beautiful in America. Doesn't that make you want to scream and stamp your little feet?"

Ellen had gone white with fury, and she looked ready to throw herself at him, clawing for his eyes, but he wagged his revolver in her face and forced her to subside.

Now Alec Ford stirred. "Hasn't there been enough talk here, Horace? Wouldn't it be better if we took Hawkins and the girl out somewhere and got the killing done?"

"You're right," Lemon said. "We've

done nothing but recount what we already know."

"Women make us run off at the mouth," Ford agreed. "Ellen is a great talker. Dare swear she's great at other things too. It'd still pleasure me to find out!"

"She isn't dead yet," Lemon chuckled.

Ford made a full laugh of it. "It's a big country out there," he agreed, "and we sure do waste it."

"If I tell you to help yourself?" Lemon queried.

"I will — I will," Ford assured him airily.

"Then the sooner the better," the big man said, giving Ellen a wicked wink. "I once heard a woman say there's no better way to go."

"You're foul!" the girl breathed.

"She's right!" Mrs Kline declared. "I will not let you awful men do what you seem to have in mind."

"Yes, you will," Horace Lemon said evenly.

"I'm going for Sheriff Dan Brightwell!"

"No, you're not, Frau Kline."

"You'll have to kill me to stop me!" the older woman went on, drawing herself up to make the most impressive figure she could amidst the rolls of redundant flesh that wobbled so visibly under her clothing.

"Tempt me not," Lemon warned. "It could so easily be arranged. But I've no wish to kill you, Frau Kline. I don't think it's necessary. All I need do is remind you of the facts that govern your life. You love your husband, you are *the* homebody, and you also cling to what you've built here. Is that correct? I can see it is. Well, a few words from me in your sheriff's ear will start the wires humming right away and before long Herr Kline will be in jail. At his age, he is never going to come out again alive. That means you will spend some very lonely declining years in a probably destitute state. Do you want that? It is avoidable."

Winifred Kline said nothing to that. Her stance seemed to collapse inwards upon itself, and her face sank chinfirst into the mound of darkly lined flesh that gathered at the bottom of her throat. Her grand gesture, like her moral person, was thus shown to be hollow at the core, and it was all too clear that she was not going to further obstruct the tigerishly smiling Lemon by word or deed. The watching Hawkins smiled sardonically to himself. He quite understood. It was not that the woman was selfish or uncaring — far from it — but Horace Lemon had pierced her where she was the most vulnerable, and Hawkins could almost hear her mind protesting that Ellen and he had got themselves into this trouble and must face the consequences. No actual responsibility for their lives devolved on her. She was responsible to heaven only for her own affairs, and justified in thinking of them alone.

A shove from Alec Ford sent Hawkins reeling slightly towards the living room's exit. Recovering, he was careful to show no resentment and, when Ellen Copperstone received much the same treatment from Horace Lemon and started rounding angrily on the big man, he seized her left cuff and drew her in beside him, ignoring the reproachful eyes that she instantly turned on him. Hawkins kept her moving, and they passed out the living room and began following the passage towards the back door. Ellen showed signs of making a real fuss now — and even flying at him in her fear — but he tugged sharply at her sleeve to enjoin silence and tried to will her to pick up his thoughts. If she would only behave, the vigilance of the men guarding them might soon decline a little; then, accepting that the prisoners would have to be taken some distance clear of town before their murders could be carried out, there was always the chance that, in the course of the walk involved, the guards would relax sufficiently to permit a sudden escape attempt. The situation would have to be right, of course — and Hawkins could not readily imagine how any such lucky circumstance might arise — but they could only travel hopefully. Still holding on to Ellen's sleeve, he sensed her new rebuke. Yes, he had only to worry about dying, but she had to consider the additional hazard that she would be violated too. He wasn't insensitive to what that could mean to a woman — even in the last minutes of her life — but he could not reveal the least hint of his sympathy right then. She must find any reassurance that was going within herself. This was a tough situation, by heaven, and she had need be strong! He couldn't do a thing for her — yet.

Leaving the house by its back door, they entered the yard behind it. Lemon steered the party towards a gate set in the fence beyond the point at which the path from the main street provided access to the rear of Adolf Kline's property. Alec Ford stepped into the land and opened the gate. He passed through it, gun in hand, and gestured for Hawkins and the girl to follow him. They had no choice, and he kept them covered while the other three members of the group came out. Then Horace Lemon called a halt and told the largest of the two hardcases who had been bringing up the rear with him — a fellow whom he named as Thomson — to latch up in their wake. This was done, and after that Lemon lighted a cigar and signalled for his party to move forward again, fragrant smoke trailing across the air as he swung his hand to the front.

Hawkins gazed ahead of them now. From the signs of building present, he guessed that the ground they were crossing had been marked out as additional lot space, but nothing had come of the new venture and the land reached out as a flat and featureless presence until it met a scattering of trees and bushes about a quarter of a mile beyond them. After that dirt and rubble sloped upwards, ascending at a fairly shallow angle to a ridge of bluntly heaving granite that appeared to mature into more substantial rock forms a short distance further on and then recede into greater outcrops of the same rugged kind along the base of the southern sky. Those far places invited, but Hawkins was not too concerned just now with features of a terrain that he could not fully see. The miles had always breathed their temptation to a riding man like him, but it was that first ridge yonder — not more than half a mile away — that fixed his interest at this minute. For if death planned to visit Ellen Copperstone and himself before long, it would most surely do so behind that initial upthrust of granite. If a pair of shots were triggered at the back of that mass, they would go virtually unheard in town, and a couple of knife-thrusts or clubbing blows to the head would be totally inaudible to the people of Rock Springs and instantly absorbed by the hanging silence of the wild. Hawkins shuddered inwardly. He had often been close to violent death, but he had never glimpsed it quite so plainly as he did now. It seemed to lack reality, and yet he knew it was horribly real.

He focused his eyes. The trees and bushes were getting close. He could see the details of their boughs and foliage. Then he glanced down abruptly, his awareness of the smaller things persisting. He watched the movements of his feet; Ellen's too; and also Alec Ford's, as the man kept surging to walk even with them. It had never really occurred to him before how different the mechanisms of walking were from one person to the next. He tended to shuffle — a horseman's lazy characteristic — Ellen minced a trifle, ever the lady, and Ford trod the earth like a big cat. The study was fascinating in its way — and he had no doubt that he would see other and no less curious variations if he looked to his rear and down — but the movements of the individual foot and leg all achieved the same result: they kept their owners moving. The party entered the bushes and trees; and then it was through them. Now the ground sloped upwards and, as the walkers climbed, the vision of a violent death became more and more deeply branded into Hawkins' imagination.

The toil on the ascent was steady but not great. They neared the summit of the ridge within two minutes. A cleft was visible in the bluntly serrated granite which ran there, and they headed for the opening and passed through it, reaching its further side without difficulty and slithering down the brief incline beyond. Now another acclivity faced them, and to the right of it, growing unsuspected and like an aspidistra in a bowl of stone, was a stand of jackpines. The lank trees, dark and dense, were an open invitation to any deed of the wickedness that a passer-by might contemplate; and, when Hawkins heard the heavy-footed Horace Lemon come to a standstill, he feared that this must be the place where it was all to end; but he soon realized that he had misunderstood the big man to that extent, for Lemon simply said: "Well, Alec, here's a secluded spot. Help yourself!"

"Thankee, Horace," Ford responded. "So I will!"

Gloating, Ford closed on Ellen Copperstone and made a grab at her. His fingers touched her right arm, but she snatched the limb out of his closing grasp and jumped away, spinning full circle while she ducked and then setting off up the slope before her at a spanking pace, her hems already lifted and dainty feet rising and falling as surely as a deer's. Crying out wrathfully, Ford went after her, though climbing with a far less accurate tread, and he kept grabbing for the bottom of her skirt and just missing.

Now that she had got fully into her stride, Ellen ascended faster yet on her slightly splayed but firmly braced legs, and the rest moved into her wake — Hawkins in a position that divided the pursuit — and he was immediately behind Alec Ford when the man lost his footing on the edge of a granite step and staggered backwards into a kind of reverse caper that saw his descending fork come to rest on the shoulders of the closely following prisoner.

The weight of the man's arrival would normally have been more than enough to topple Hawkins backwards and send them both rolling down to the bottom of the grade behind them; but the prisoner had the split second presence of mind to perceive that he had just been gifted with a golden opportunity. Catching his own threatened collapse with the strength of his back and legs, he crouched there for a moment with Ford's lower person draped around his neck. Then, straightening with every ounce of force that he could generate, he sent Ford catapulting off his shoulders and into the space immediately behind him, where he arrived like a missile among the three pursuing members of the Lemon party which included the boss himself. Ford's momentum knocked the trio off their feet and flung them into reverse somersaults. After that they spun downwards to the foot of the slope and came to rest in a formless sprawl of limbs and bodies.

Knowing that he had achieved something that must prove fairly devastating, Hawkins seized the edge of the granite step off which Ford had first slipped backwards and glanced at each of the figures spreadeagled below in turn. All four were stirring — Ford the most strongly — but Hawkins could see that they were to a man badly dazed and would not be moving around too sharply for a few minutes. Important as chasing their quarry must be to them, they should prove too badly stunned to reorientate themselves and renew the hunt before the fugitives had crossed the next ridge and passed from their sight.

Hawkins felt a momentary exaltation that was somehow less than relief. Then he went scrambling upwards in Ellen Copperstone's tracks as fast as he could go. The girl was already several yards beyond him and showed no sign of looking back. He grunted his approval. She was taking care of herself, and that was all he asked. The Fates had been good to them, and they must not throw their luck away in undue concern for each other. They were already out of reach of all but gunshots from below, and he couldn't see any of those flying in their direction before they had reached complete safety.

But it was invariably the same. Even that moment of confidence was one too many. Down there a pistol started to crack and boom, and lead rang and flew across the immediate face of the ridge. The shooting was hopelessly inaccurate, and not one of the bullets fired struck anywhere near the girl or Hawkins himself. But you could never tell where ricochets would fly, and suddenly Ellen cried out and twisted to rest in a sitting position on the grade above.

6

SHOCKED cold by what had just happened, Hawkins dug in his toes and clawed for handholds among the rocks and outcrops about him, climbing like a man possessed, and he reached Ellen Copperstone almost before she could lift her face from examining herself and register his presence. "Have you been hit?" he panted, glancing back and down to where Alec Ford was resting on his left hip and creased above the empty six-shooter which now lay smoking between his raised thighs.

"No," the girl responded breathlessly. "I've twisted my ankle. A bullet flew past my head and caused me to lose my footing."

"Can you walk?"

"I believe so," she answered. "I don't think it's a bad sprain. Just a momentary pang."

"I hope that's all it is," Hawkins breathed, helping her up. "Put your weight on me if you need to. Alec Ford has emptied his gun, but there are three others down there. Let's get over the summit. We can worry about all the rest when we've found a place to hide up."

"Is there such a place?" she wondered, passing a rather despairing eye across the shapes of stone that reared about them.

"Gotta be one somewhere," he promised. "There always is. Come on! Let's make tracks before that bunch down there pull round. Unhappily, they ain't dead."

They resumed climbing. Hawkins had his left arm around the girl's shoulders, and she leaned in against his chest each time she put her weight on her left foot. He could already see swelling at the ankle of her calfskin boot — and he realized that she must have sustained a worse sprain than she had suggested — but he was also sure, from her immediate performance, that her ankle was not broken and that she would probably be able to get around unaided once it had been properly strapped up. But you needed strong bandages to provide that kind of support and, so far as he could see, they would have nothing but strips torn from her lace petticoat to use. Always supposing, indeed, that they were given the chance to treat her injury at all.

Hawkins kept an eye to his rear. The men below were still largely immobile, but Ford was on his feet and the other two hardcases resting on their knees. Fortunately — since the chase would certainly have resumed at this juncture had it been otherwise — Horace Lemon was the one man still stretched out on his back, but there was enough movement in his body to show that, if he had been knocked near enough senseless, his true injuries were, like those of his companions, no more than superficial. The men would all be on their feet before long and, if slow at first when they began ascending again, would still be an ever-present threat to keep the pressure on a quarry which had also been slowed down by a hurt. The balance which had shifted so far in favour of the fugitives could now tilt back in the other direction, and it was hard for Hawkins to see how the girl and he were to make their ultimate escape.

The escapers pressed on and upwards. Hawkins supplied most of the willpower needed to keep them in motion. They reached the rimrock, he sweating copiously and the girl distressed, only to discover that the crest itself was eight feet of vertical granite which the seasons had bevelled at the top. It was a far more formidable obstacle than it had looked from lower down and, even if Hawkins and Ellen had been at their fittest, scrambling over it would have been out of the question. Drawing the injured girl to the right, Hawkins began skirting the summit — seeking a way through — and, luckily, it was not long before another of those rifts like the one which they had used lower down presented itself and they were able to pass through the granite crest and start descending the slope of encrusted grit and sand at the other side of it.

Still standing higher than most of the country around them, Hawkins was able to absorb all the main characteristics of the terrain south-wards. He saw that they were nearing an area which was naturally divided by several parallel walls of rock — running between east and west — which appeared to enclose small valleys between them.

Not much encouraged by the scene, Hawkins eventually perceived that the outlook was worse than he had imagined, since each one of the partitioning bluffs on view seemed impermeable to the traveller and there was simply no miracle that he could perform to change this apparently unobliging country into a more co-operative terrain.

Bracing still, he did what seemed to him the only thing he could and helped his companion down into the low immediately beneath them. Here he turned her to the left and into the start of a walk that he feared would, from all the signs, lead them to boxing cliffs and a dead end. Obviously daunted — for though she was in some pain Ellen Copperstone remained no less aware than he — the girl promptly suggested that they should face in the opposite direction and then take their chance. But Hawkins' observations from higher up had already satisfied him that the valley's western end was completely walled in by almost perpendicular stone, and, as he went on steering her eastwards, he reminded Miss Copperstone that they had only to make the wrong choice of direction and Horace Lemon and his hirelings would need to do no more, after they had crossed the ridge, than cut off their return and take them prisoner again — with a likely repetition of what had been planned earlier for her. Ellen had little more to say about the matter after that.

They continued making the best progress they could, but it was impossible to forget that they had merciless pursuers behind them, and Hawkins was not surprised, when a distant sound echoed out of their wake, to look back for what must have been the twentieth time and at last see Lemon and company at the top of the tracks which he and the girl had left on the slope which they had most recently descended. The villains were moving freely again and, in fact, only a few hundred yards behind them. Hawkins felt the hand of fear return coldly to grip the pit of his stomach. He felt oddly cheated. The enemy seemed to be catching them up more quickly than ought to be the case. He had been counting, at least subconsciously, on a longer respite. Yet he knew that in reality Lemon and his men had been slow about it. Pistols banged, and the explosions echoed around the rock masses that enclosed them. Hawkins thought he heard a bullet fall, but he judged that Ellen and he were being fired on to give them a scare. It would be an out and out accident if a slug scored a hit at the present range. Yet the explosions conveyed an imperative too. The fugitives must go faster. If only Ellen were still capable of running. But only he was able to do that now.

There was nothing for it. "I've got to carry you," he said. "Like that I can run!"

"All right," she gulped. "I don't mind piggy-back."

But that wasn't quite what he had in mind. Bending, he swept Ellen up across his shoulders. She uttered a little cry at this lack of ceremony, but offered no real objection. If an apology was due, Hawkins decided it would have to wait until later. He set off at a full run, with the girl bouncing up and down across his bent back. He was far from fresh, but Ellen was of no great weight and, inspired by the chill in his entrails, he pounded westwards up the floor of the valley at a pace that wasn't much below his best. He kept it up too — for the better part of half a mile — and, when the burning in his lungs and the pounding of his heart did force him to slow up, he still managed to keep going at a speed which he knew the men behind him would find hard to match.

The odd shot still popped back there. Soon, however, the valley cornered to the right and carried the fugitives out of their hunters' sight. Hawkins ran onwards for a further two hundred yards. Now the walls fell back into a semi-circle and the place opened up and seemed to spread considerably, with the uneven floor revealing large traces of stepped erosion, boulder-piles appearing close to tumbling, and pyramids of scree piling around the plinths of miniature buttes which the ages had formed round and about; but the wonderful chaos of the scene did little more than register with Hawkins; for, as he shook the sweat from his eyes and peered around him — he sought a possible hiding place on the right from which he might eventually succeed in doubling back eastwards if the seekers should by-pass him; but there seemed no cover present of a kind that would serve his purpose with any real degree of certainty.

"Put me down, Sam," Ellen Copperstone ordered. "Now you've got us into a fine mess, haven't you?"

"Could be worse," he said defiantly, gently setting her down on her feet; and then he explained to her about trying to double back.

"Sam," she commented acidly, "you're a man of great optimism."

"Ellen, I'll never just roll over and die — that's for certain."

"No," she then surprised him by saying, "you're no coward, and you're as safe as any man to be around."

"Humph!" he grunted. "We should

have met before this."

"We've been worlds apart."

In every meaning of it, yes. "Well, we aren't any more," he confided. "Better late than never."

"It could be too late, Sam."

He recalled how he had felt when she had kissed that polecat Wellard. "Only if we let it be. Let's seek for some place marvellous to hide."

Words could be treacherous and a guy said many stupid things in the course of his life — always without meaning to and usually without realizing it — but Hawkins admitted to himself that his last utterance would need a heap of beating for sheer inanity. "Some place marvellous", eh? At this spot, where the Ages revealed their fullest ruin? But, fortunately, Ellen Copperstone either hadn't noticed his latest asinine braying or was tired of remarking his foolishness, and she had begun casting around her — her movements afflicted by a nasty limp — and was obviously seeking as he had so strongly urged. He sighed, dashing a sleeve across his brow. They had two or three minutes at most. What were they going to find anyhow? What was there for them to find? She had spoken of his optimism; but he knew that his confidence was little more than a natural brashness. They were trapped, and that was that.

"Sam!"

"What?"

"Over here."

She was standing close to the foot of the cliff on their right. He walked over and joined her. "What?" he repeated.

"Doesn't that look like the end of a once-used path to you?" she inquired, pointing to where, a few feet up from the base of the bluff and approached by a ramp of sorts, a small taking-off place of long-ago jammed in dust and rubble suggested a spot that had been regularly trodden by human feet. Hawkins raised his eyebrows, grinning inwardly, for his mind was already seeking some form of mild sarcasm with which to put her down; but then he found himself almost physically biting his tongue to keep silent, for there was no question that what she had spotted could indicate the place where an all but invisible path had once emerged from behind the rock wall adjacent. Anyway, the girl had given proof that she possessed a remarkably sharp pair of eyes and deserved his serious attention if nothing else.

Hawkins moved right up to the face of the cliff. Treading on the ramp, he lifted himself up and peered into the break that he now saw in the stone before him. Amazingly, his imagination was fulfilled and there was a path of sorts behind the rockface. It was in fact the floor of another of those rifts with which the area had been so liberally bespattered by the tremors of a cooling earth untold millions of years ago, and he was fairly sure that, if Ellen and he entered it, they would at worst be able to continue their flight in the valley beyond this one and at best might even seem to vanish from the path of their hunters and elude them for good; since the men back there — recently shaken up and undoubtedly animated at this time by a rampant impatience — would be unlikely to either think clearly enough or concentrate hard enough to locate this spot for themselves today. "Quick, Ellen!" Hawkins ordered, slipping into the concealed gap himself and then extending a hand to her.

Ellen's fingers tightened about his, and he drew her into the opening, where she reeled weakly against the stone on her left and sagged there in a moment of near collapse, looking at him intently and listening anxiously towards the ground from which she had come. "What's up?" he demanded, releasing her hand.

"Horace and his men were just coming round the corner as you pulled me in here," she explained breathlessly. "They could have seen me."

"Damn!" he exclaimed without heat,

cocking his own right ear and putting it acutely to work.

"Must you, Sam?"

"What's in a 'damn'?"

"More than you think!" Ellen protested. "It reflects your mind!"

"Hogwash!" he sniffed, giving her a narrow, floppy-eared look that made him feel a mongrel all the same. "You're too fine tuned, dear Ellen! Do come on! Seems to me you weren't spotted. We'll soon find out anyhow, and waiting here could prove fatal."

He sidled off swiftly to his right, forgetting the girl's disability, and she hopped after him, trying to hide her pained expression. Hawkins was sorry for his latest lack of consideration, but didn't really feel that it warranted notice, and he was still forcing her to come along at a pace that was much faster than she could comfortably manage, when the rift ceased defiling for him and he emerged on valley grass, seeing, to his right and not a hundred yards away, a waterhole enclosed by trees and a clapboard shack with a tarpaper roof and filthy windows. The building had obviously seen better days and was going to collapse before long; but its very presence bespoke humankind and had an uplifting influence because of it.

Hawkins waited for Ellen to catch up with him. She soon did that, and he helped her into the open, renewing his support by putting an arm around her body. After that he nodded towards the nearby shack and said sardonically: "Home sweet home."

"For somebody — once, I suppose," Ellen said, turning her head and gazing back along the rift which carried the makeshift path towards its fairly distant ingress. "I do believe we're all right, Sam. I don't think they saw me after all."

"Reckon not," he agreed. "They'd have been coming through here before now."

They held their ground for a minute or two longer all the same — making as sure as possible that all was indeed well for them just now — and then, by a kind of tacit agreement, they headed for the clearly derelict shack, since Hawkins realized that, although an obvious risk still persisted and could manifest before all was done, his companion needed to rest more than anything else; and he too, of course, was no longer fresh enough to carry the girl upon his back as he had before. They would just have to keep their eyes open and hope to goodness that, as he had thought likely, their pursuers would prove too shaky and careless in their search at the other side of the cliff to light upon the hidden path that led here. It was taking a chance, yes, but what else had they been doing from the outset?

With Ellen limping heavily and Hawkins now feeling a much greater concern for her injury than he had earlier on, they walked across to the shack and pushed inside, the door rocking loosely on its hinges as it swung-to behind them. The tiny building reeked of damp and animal visitations; but, when closed up to the full, it still seemed reasonably tight against the weather. Looking around him, Hawkins reckoned that, as nearly as he could judge it, the original furniture was still present. There was a low wooden bunk against the back wall, and upon it a mouldy mattress lay. A pot-bellied stove stood in an angle of the single room. There was a table not far from it that was just large enough for a man to eat at or work on, and a broken rocking chair lay upon its back under the window behind it. The contents of a work basket had been scattered across the floor, and a mirror — which was in fact a square of polished tin — hung crookedly upon the shanty's eastern wall above a wooden stand that supported a rusty tin bowl. Altogether, the interior of the little building was a begrimed and depressing sight — and Ellen Copperstone shuddered at it — but the bunk, with all its shortcomings, gave her somewhere to sit, and she sank down with a sobbing gasp and stretched out her sprained ankle until the foot to which it belonged rested on the overturned work basket.

Kneeling, Hawkins untied and carefully removed the girl's left boot, indicating then that she should roll her stocking down. This she did, and he examined the injured joint. With the corseting boot removed, the swelling seemed to have ballooned, and bathing in cold water was clearly the best method of controlling it; so, going to the tin bowl that stood upon the wooden stand, he inspected it for holes and, finding it sound, carried it outside and filled it at the waterhole. After that he brought it back indoors and placed it where the girl could immerse her sprain in liquid. "Oh, that's much better," she murmured. "Thank you, Sam."

"You're welcome," he assured her, smiling. "Let your foot stay in the water for a time. I'll do my best to bandage your ankle later on. I'm afraid you'll have to sacrifice your petticoat. You'll have to tear it up into some good broad strips for me."

"Very well," Ellen said. "Will you mind stepping outside?"

"While you take your dress off?" Hawkins queried. "Not a bit. Sing out when you want me to come back inside."

Ellen nodded. "It's turned out worse than I expected."

"You could have broken it," he reminded, moving to the door. "It's not busted."

"No, it isn't," she agreed thankfully, studying him wide-eyed as he checked on the threshold. "I — I thought it was all up with us at — at those pine trees, didn't — didn't you?"

"We survived," he said, "and that's what we'll keep on doing."

She gave her head another jerk. Hawkins walked clear of the door and away to his left. Tucking his thumbs into the top of his trousers, he kicked his way past the tree-girt waterhole and out to the tussocky ground beyond it. Here he halted, well within earshot of the shack and in full view of the ridges and bluffs which filled the eastern scene from this spot. He could just make out the faintest of tracks snaking up the grade at the valley's end and then threading some rock jaws at the summit of the ground in that direction, and he had the notion that a route into Rock Springs still existed over there. If so, they weren't entirely hemmed in, as he had feared they might be, and the dim path might still prove a convenience later on.

Turning about once more, Hawkins looked towards the defile that ran along the back of the rock wall on his left. Everything over there was in shadow and remained as still as the grave. He wondered whether Lemon and company were still hunting for him and Ellen Copperstone in the half circle of ruin beyond this point, and he was tempted to go and see; but somewhere in his mind a superstitious warning triggered itself and he decided to leave well alone. It also occurred to him now that the light was fading all around the valley's rims. Night was not that far off. The hours of the day had gone past at such a hectic rate that he had hardly been aware of them. Heck but he was hungry, and thirsty too. While he could do something about the latter — which he did by returning to the waterhole and drinking his fill from the water there out of cupped hands — he could do nothing about the former. He imagined that what was true for him in this matter must also be true for Ellen. Admittedly, the girl had been in pain for some time — and pain suppressed appetite — but even so she needed to keep a lining on her stomach. But he couldn't see much chance of their getting a meal before tomorrow morning. And then they'd have to be lucky — and probably sly about it too.

"Sam!" The summons came as a muffled call from the shack.

Hawkins walked back to the shanty and ducked inside it. He saw Ellen sitting much as he had left her. Her injured ankle was still immersed in the cold water which the rusty bowl contained, but three broad and carefully torn strips of lace lay beside her on the bunk, proof that she had actually undressed during his absence and torn up a large portion of her petticoat to produce the bandages that now lay ready for use.

Nodding his approval, Hawkins picked up one piece of the binding material and used it to dry Ellen's foot. Then he went to work with the other two strips and bandaged her sprained ankle as tightly and correctly as he knew how, ending up a few minutes later with a job that didn't look too bad and just about satisfied him. "Nigh enough," he commented, secretly feeling a little proud of his handiwork; and then, emitting a grunt, he rose from the kneeling position which he had occupied while playing doctor and brushed off his knees. "That ankle's sure blown up, girl. It's the deuce of a size! I can't see you walking far on it. Not tonight anyhow."

"I'm afraid you're right," Ellen confessed, frowning thoughtfully. "Do you think Horace and his men have stopped looking for us and gone back to Rock Springs yet?"

"Doubt it," Hawkins responded, his thoughts jumping abruptly to a new track. "Is it my horse you're thinking of? I could sneak into town and fetch it when the dark descends. The poor critter will have to bear us both, but it's our best bet for clearing the district and getting back to the waggons. I reckon you're game for that, eh?"

"It isn't quite what I had in mind, Sam."

"Oh?"

"Didn't Horace Lemon say that my jewels were lying in Adolf Kline's safe?" the girl inquired earnestly. "If Horace hasn't been back to town since escorting us this way, they could still be there.

You could ask Adolf for them on my behalf, could you not? Your horse would still be waiting afterwards."

"To hell with you and your baubles!" Hawkins snorted, feeling that his companion wished to use him in a dangerous fashion. "What will you do next?"

"But, Sam," the girl protested with a beguiling gentleness, "for me the jewels are what it's all about. Don't you understand that?"

He understood it only too well. A girl who had been rich must find it a sickener to be poor. But it would be easy to risk his neck for her once too often.

"If my brother-in-law Horace gets his hands on those jewels," Ellen persisted, her seriousness intensifying to the limit, "he will have won. It will be the end of all my chances. Do you want that? Please see my point of view."

"I do see it," Hawkins answered, sympathetic enough but still tightly on the defensive.

"Do it for me, Sam," Ellen urged firmly. "However all this turns out, you won't lose by it."

Hawkins studied her face in the gathering shadows. It was pale and pleading, false in some sense — for her promise had to be specious and conditional — but he wanted her now: wanted her to keep for his; and he had no doubt, as by the sudden process of emotional maturing which had overtaken him during the day, that what she required of him here was the essential price of any future relationship which might develop between them. If he played her keeper tonight, and put on a masterful show of force, he would gain nothing in the long run — even if he achieved his own professional ends now. He knew instinctively that Ellen was prepared to bargain but, regardless of anything that she might have started to feel for him, would make no free gifts. Her great beauty masked a tough and wilful woman, one who would never count the world well lost for love.

Hawkins perceived that if he wanted Ellen Copperstone, he might as well accept this facet of her nature once and for all. "Okay," he said, sighing resignedly. "I'll see what I can do."

7

WITH a tall sunset sky stained red at his back and fingers of shadow that were black as crêpe lying across the grass around the waterhole, Hawkins left the shack and walked towards the advancing gloom of the night. He followed the dim path which he had earlier detected on the valley's eastern floor and, bowing into his steps, climbed with the climbing land. Arriving at the jaws of stone atop the summit for which he had been heading, he passed through them and began his descent on the other side. Now, his eyes shifting a quarter turn to the right, he made out lights burning well back on a corridor of flatter land which formed the stem of a cross upon the band of more rugged going which lay between him and what had to be the position of

Rock Springs. The lights drew him like magnets — even when his path settled low and he could no longer make out the physical presence of their glitter through windows at which the drapes had still to be drawn — and, striding forward with more determination than actual vigour, he cut the trail that led into the town's western end within twenty minutes and entered the place itself within five more, passing the law office and his drooping horse as he went on that little bit further up the main street and came to Adolf Kline's house of business.

So far Hawkins had met nobody who had taken any notice of him, and he hadn't in fact clapped eyes on anybody that he recognised; so he figured that he would keep on behaving in a natural manner and simply walk in at Kline's street door and deal with the man as any other customer might. The snag was, of course, that he might find the establishment closed by this hour — and that would obviously force a slight change of plan — but he found the door of the shop still open when he tried it and went straight into the trade room itself, making out Kline's counter, grille, scales and safe in the gloom at the back of the musty smelling space and wondering why no lamp had been lighted as yet.

Feeling unable to stand still, Hawkins paced the floor boards for half a minute — hoping that the noise he thus made would bring Kline into the shop — but nobody entered through the door at the left rear of the place and his patience finally gave out and he hammered loudly on the counter with his fist. "Anybody there?" he shouted. "Customer!"

The echoes shrank back at once into what Hawkins believed was the same silence from which they had arisen. But then he heard a faint noise from the house behind the shop and he tilted his head and listened intently. The sound repeated. It was human and tearful. Somebody back there — Mrs Kline, he suspected — was crying pitifully. His call had undoubtedly provoked this response, and he had to hear in it some kind of plea for help. So, without more ado, he threw up his left leg and vaulted over the counter, landing cleanly enough on the other side; and then he turned towards the door on his left and passed through it into the house itself, spotting a shaft of lamplight in the passage ahead of him that emerged from the remembered position of Mrs Kline's parlour. "You there, ma'am?" he asked tentatively.

The sobbing became louder, and there could no longer be any question about its being a plea. Lengthening his stride, Hawkins entered the living room and saw the fleshy figure of Mrs Kline collapsed beside an armchair in which the bulky, white-maned shape of an ageing man with a crumpled Germanic face was slumped back, his arms dangling and his legs thrust out before him. The old fellow was clearly gasping the last of his life away, and a circle of blood that covered the front of his white shirt told that he had been shot close to the heart. Removing his neckerchief, Hawkins lunged instinctively towards the wound, aiming to staunch it, but he had yet to touch the bloody hole, when the old man's throat rattled and he sagged into the final collapse of death. Checking now and stepping back again, Hawkins uttered a murmur of regret and began replacing his neckerchief with fingers that had become slow and fumbling. "Who did it?" he asked of the sobbing woman, whose face was almost touching the floor and who did not appear to have witnessed the passing of the man in the chair. "He's gone, you know."

Mrs Kline picked up her torso and then threw back her head, uttering a long howl which ended with her dropping her chin on the dead man's right knee and looking up into his now unmoving features. "Adolf!" she moaned. "Adolf!"

"Who did it?" Hawkins repeated, deciding that he must prompt her somewhat. "Another visit from Horace Lemon and his misfits?"

"No," Mrs Kline gulped, sitting back on the fireside mat and turning her face up and round to look at the man standing between her and the door. "It was Ellen's young man — Jason Wellard. Who — who would believe it?"

"I would," Hawkins growled sardonically. "So that young bastard has put his sticky fingers into this pot! Well, it's a hanging job, ma'am, and I'll see he hangs. Or that he pays for what he's done. A life for a life, eh?"

"A life for a life," Mrs Kline agreed, letting Hawkins help her to her feet. "He came in from the street, you know, and simply demanded Ellen Copperstone's jewels. I — I heard him in the shop, and — and went through to — to see . . . "

"Reckon I get the picture, ma'am," Hawkins acknowledged harshly, studying the newly dead Adolf Kline's wound with an experienced eye. "It couldn't have happened long ago."

"Not quarter of an hour," the woman replied. "The young man left the shop only minutes before you came in. It was all so — so cold-blooded." She shook her head, blinking at new tears. "Adolf opened the safe — he kept a pistol inside it, do you see? — and he snatched the gun out and pointed it at Mr Wellard, telling him to take himself off; but Jason Wellard drew a gun from inside his coat and shot my husband where he stood. Adolf was not the kind to fire on another human being."

"What a pity he wasn't!" Hawkins gritted. "If he had been, your husband would have still been alive now and Wellard most likely pointed feet-first at Boot Hill. God-dammit! Why does everything have to get worse and worse? This will play the devil with Ellen, when she hears of it. Your husband — the good friend of her family — murdered by the man she lately adored. 'Cos lately's the word now, that's for sure!" He sucked in the deepest of breaths. "Can you manage here, Mrs Kline? I'm off right now to nail Wellard's hide to the nearest barn door!"

"Do it, please," Mrs Kline said, pulling herself together with an effort that seemed to perfectly complement her next words. "This is my tragedy, son, and I must find the way to live through it."

"Betcha," he agreed as kindly as he could. "Do you happen to know where Wellard was staying? Would it have been the Forkland hotel?"

"Why, no," Mrs Kline responded. "I don't think so. I was in town during the afternoon and I saw him come out of the Teton hotel. That's on the other side of the street and just a few doors east of here."

"Thank you," Hawkins said. "I think I know the building you mean. I'll try it anyhow." He snapped a finger and thumb. "One thing more, ma'am. Where's your husband's gun?"

"He dropped it on the floor of the shop," the woman answered, "when he was hit by the bullet and the jewel box taken."

Hawkins lifted a finger in salute. Then he left the woman to her parlour and her grief for the dead man. Going back into the shop, he searched around on the dark floor behind the counter until he located Adolf Kline's fallen revolver with a kicking foot. Picking the weapon up, he took out and struck a match in order to make sure the pistol was carrying a full load; and, finding the cylinder loaded in all chambers, he shook out his tiny light and holstered the sixgun, feeling fully dressed again as its weight dragged a trifle at his gunbelt. After that he vaulted the counter once again and stepped back onto the street, turning right on the sidewalk and starting another of his rough calculations as he fixed his gaze upon a large building across the way which had a short, steep roof of tiles, four floors, a slightly pretentious portico, and numerous draped windows behind which shadows moved in the lamplight. The black silhouette of the structure seemed to float a foot or two above ground level, and Hawkins knew that it was the Teton hotel all right.

His mind was still adding things up. If Wellard had indeed been staying yonder, he'd had time since killing Adolf Kline and stealing the Copperstone jewels to have got his things together and paid his bill. It figured that he would not hang around a second longer than he had to, so he could already be galloping one direction or another into the countryside. Or he could be round the back of the hotel and getting his horse out of the stables there. There was the third possibility, too, that he might be heading up the main street towards the livery barn, where he could equally have lodged his mount. Three possibilities, yes, and they could all be wrong — for Wellard's route into Wyoming appeared to have followed the railroad and he could have arrived here by train — but it was necessary that Hawkins gamble on one of his notions being correct; so which should he choose?

Frankly tired, he could not make up his mind and might have lapsed into a form of paralysis had a hurrying figure not suddenly passed through the light from a street flare burning at an intersection about a hundred and fifty yards beyond him. The sight instantly got him moving eastwards, for the livery barn was situated near the top end of the main street. He could not be sure that he had just glimpsed Jason Wellard, but the guy so briefly visible had certainly appeared a lot taller than most and been acting as he would have expected a man with new blood on his hands to act. The fact of synchronicity also entered into the matter. For when a fugitive was known to be around, he wasn't usually so difficult to pick out even in a crowd and, in an empty place like the Rock Springs of this hour, it was a whole lot easier — allowing for the town lighting — for there was little more than the night itself to hide the guilty one. Anyway, the hurrying man was definitely one to pursue on spec. If it should turn out that he had acted in error, then he was probably going to get it wrong by this time whatever he did.

Excitement renewed itself in Hawkins and his fatigue seemed to melt away. He shortened his steps, speeding up almost to a run and, as he narrowed the gap between his quarry and himself, he glimpsed the tall man several times in the light from flare or window and became increasingly convinced that his rather snap judgment of a short while ago had not been at fault. He was ninety nine percent certain that it was Jason Wellard moving ahead of him and that the young man was carrying a big carpetbag in his right hand and a box of some kind under his left arm. The box could as easily be a jewel case — or protection for a jewel case — as anything else. Its presence alone made the continued pursuit a must.

Three lanterns, placed high on beams of timber and burning brightly, appeared on the right. The collective glow revealed the blackly gaping door and even broader frontage of a large wooden building that Hawkins knew to be the livery barn. Here came the crucial test. Would the man in front now turn into the yard before the commercial stables? He did so, head bowed and his presence more furtive than ever and, as the light from the three lanterns fell directly upon him, revealing his blond hair, he was shown to be Jason Wellard beyond any further shadow of a doubt. Already close enough to shout a challenge, Hawkins desisted in the hope of avoiding an exchange of gunfire — or any other kind of fight — for he reckoned that, if he could get right up close, the presence of a pistol at the other's back or ribs would achieve all that was required. Beyond that, Hawkins didn't doubt that Sheriff Dan Brightwell, once apprised of what had occurred in Adolf Kline's shop, would be glad to supply a good strong cell in which to hold Wellard until such time as the law could try and hang him.

Turning right on reaching the nearer limit of the livery barn's front yard, Hawkins approached the building itself at a rapid tiptoe, ending up with his right shoulder pressed against the doorpost on that side and his revolver drawn and poised. Inching half of his face into the space beyond, he peered round into the closer parts of the dimly lighted stables, seeing Jason Wellard speaking animatedly with an ostler at the top of the first aisle there. The young man was apparently getting an argument from the liveryman, and he looked on the verge of losing his temper. Then, in a clear effort to control himself, he jerked his face round towards the night, his gaze centring upon the exact spot from where his pursuer was peeping in at him. He blanched, perceiving himself unexpectedly threatened, then threw a glance about him in the plain hope of seeing some quick solution to his latest problem; and, with the devil always seeming to take care of his own, there was one present at the opposite side of the barn and in line with him, where a well-dressed gentleman was just receiving his newly saddled horse from the hands of a second ostler and making ready to leave the premises.

Ever the opportunist, it seemed, Wellard thrust aside the liveryman to whom he had been speaking and dashed across the width of the barn, arriving at speed between the second ostler and the gentleman who was in the act of mounting his horse. He shoved the liveryman to the floor with a push to the right; then tearing the gentleman from his nearside stirrup by grabbing him round the waist, flung him upon his back also. After that, catching up the reins of his third victim's mount — but dropping his carpetbag and the box he was carrying in the process — he swung astride the animal and kicked it straight ahead for the main street.

Hawkins had already dived into the middle of the barn's great doorway. He came to a complete standstill as he saw Wellard aim the already charging horse straight at him. Loth to shoot, with other folk around and the risk of a ricochet always present, Hawkins essayed a wild swipe — hoping to divert the onrushing animal from its course — but the horse was scared and its jaws being firmly held. It was a large form and full of energy, and Hawkins realized in the moment left to him that a blow from his gun barrel would have no effect on it at all, so he made a vigorous effort to spring aside, bending as far to the right as he could manage at the same time. The horse kept coming flat out, and he was within inches of avoiding it completely, but its left shoulder nevertheless caught him with force enough to send him whirling across the floor. Inevitably, he lost his balance during the spin and down he went, measuring his length with the other supine figures present. But, as his senses clouded, he was only too aware that Wellard was clear, away, and unlikely to be caught tonight on the easterly course that he appeared to have chosen as he turned on to the main street.

Rising gingerly to his feet after a minute or so — for he had been struck quite hard and realized that he could have been hurt more than he had imagined — Hawkins thrust the revolver that he was still gripping into his holster and then bore down hard upon his knees with his hands, breathing steadily until his brain cleared fully and he could be sure that all was well with him otherwise. Straightening up after that, Hawkins glanced around him and saw that the two ostlers — already on their feet — had gone to the still supine gentleman and were preparing to help him up. He watched them at it for a moment, gathering from their fawning attention and sympathetic remarks that their dizzy charge was a figure of some importance hereabouts, then returned to his own affairs, picking up the box which Jason Wellard had dropped and carrying it aside.

The box was a lightly made thing. Hawkins held it against his body in the crook of his arm. Unhooking the brass catches that held down its lid of Japanese lacquerwork, he opened the box up and, as he had thought might prove the case, found a second and more ornate box inside it. This was constructed of sandalwood and inlaid with ivory and gold. It opened when a little pressure was applied to a spring at the front of its lid. Inside the box lay diamond, ruby, and emerald necklaces, rings, both ear and finger, and a tiara which must be worth a fortune by itself, not to mention other items of less obvious value. No expert in these matters — and unable to place even an approximate worth on the jewellery encased here — Hawkins was nevertheless certain that the new start which Ellen Copperstone had seemed to be so earnestly seeking was present. If she could get anything like the trade value of the stones before him, he was pretty confident that she would never have to worry where the rent or her next meal were coming from for the rest of her days. Further, if she were blessed with an aptitude for business, here was the capital to start up almost any enterprise that appealed to her. She had only to get this jewel box to California and the worst of her troubles should be over. But he had to carry the damned thing out of here yet — and that might not be so easy.

Hawkins darted a glance to his right. The ostlers were still brushing down their customer in the broadcloth suit. The three men yonder did not appear to have any interest in him as yet, and he believed they were hardly conscious of his presence. The results of what had lately occurred remained more important to them than the reason why the violence had flared up. But the question of cause must soon supplant that of effort in their minds, and then they were going to start asking questions. He knew how persistent people could get at the first sign of evasion, and the men present would need only to see the contents of the jewel box and he was certain that he would not be allowed to leave the livery stables with Ellen Copperstone's property. Indeed, getting out of here would become about as difficult as getting out of the Territorial pen. It seemed wiser to him, as he reasoned thus, that he should melt away while the interest of the men across the floor was otherwise absorbed.

Experience had taught him that his best chance always lay in doing a thing like this slowly and casually — for the guy who called least attention to himself obviously got away with most — so he sauntered out of the door, crossed the front yard at a strolling pace, while angling out of the light from the overhanging lanterns as craftily as possible, then began moving westwards. He was actually some yards along the boardwalk, when a shout went up from behind him and a harsh voice that could only belong to one of the ostlers ordered him to "stop and come back here, blast your thievin' eyes!" But, having achieved the part of his exit that mattered most, Hawkins had no intention of surrendering the advantage gained and, leaving the sidewalk, he stretched into a run on the surface of the street itself. This was uneven enough to be sure, but still more trustworthy than the frequently broken slats of the boardwalk, and he soon built up enough pace to carry him rapidly towards the centre of Rock Springs and the greater silhouettes looming there against the star-strung heavens.

Hawkins imagined that he was doing enough. He thought it unlikely that he would be chased. So he just kept legging it down the edge of the way, and it was only when he heard feet stumble in his wake that he bothered to throw back a glance and so discover, as one of the men from the livery barn touched another of those bars of sudden lamplight, that he was being pursued hotfoot. Clutching the jewel box tighter, Hawkins swore under his breath and asked himself why in blazes, on this of all nights, his actions should arouse the curiosity of an apparent nonentity to the degree that the fellow — presumably the one who had already called on him to stop — should be prepared to do what his breed was supposed never to do and begin the serious burning up of energy to satisfy a vague suspicion. Blast the guy for not having the decency to conform to the ordinary! He would have to be eluded. If he once caught up, and began shouting the odds to everybody in earshot, the very situation would pertain on the main street that Hawkins most wished to avoid.

He entered a patch of darkness, but had already spotted an alley coming up on his left. Veering abruptly, he sprang across the sidewalk and entered the opening, flinging himself down the passage beyond it. Fortunately for him, the ground ahead proved free of every obstacle and his feet went on falling cleanly. This enabled him to reach the town's southern lots without making any loud noises. Now he turned right and, again running westwards and breasting through airs that were shot with errant lamplight from the rear windows of the houses nearby, planned a return to the main street much closer to the position of the law office, where his horse should still be waiting for him. Presently he craned, in order to make sure that his ploy had been successful — which appeared to have been the case — and then he pelted onwards for about another hundred yards before turning into one of the more westerly alleys and covering the final yards of his latest dash along the lots.

He emerged on the main street, checking. His legs felt suddenly weak and his knees were trembling. Grabbing a nearby verandah post, he hung on tightly. There was sweat dribbling off his temples again, and his heart was almost kicking out of his ribs. He was fit to drop and nigh done in. To hell with this for a healthy pastime! But the sheriff's office was situated only about thirty yards to his left, and he could see where his mount was standing hitched. The horse tossed its head, appearing to sense his presence. He'd be glad to climb back into the saddle. Horses had four legs and were built for running. They even enjoyed it. The bearded gentry with all the brains maintained that Man had also been built for running. Well, maybe. But there was a fellow here who'd had enough of it. Hawkins' one ambition now was to carry this box of jewels safely to the shack in which he had left Ellen Copperstone nursing her sprained ankle. His horse could do the running, and he'd do the riding. It sounded like a division of labour that would suit him very nicely. If that made him a lazy son-of-a-dog — too bad!

He stepped out into the street. His movement was greeted by another of those harsh yells from no great distance to the east of him. Great leaping Godfrey! Would that man from the livery stables never give up? Had he anticipated Hawkins' reappearance at this end of town and just kept coming when his quarry had taken to the lots? It was possible. But more likely the guy had just charged blindly on when finding himself baffled, as folk did. Though he could even be bent on paying the sheriff a visit. The varmint was plainly more canny than most — but Hawkins didn't intend to let that benefit the other in any way tonight.

His again hurrying legs brought him to his horse. Freeing the creature's head, he stepped up as best he could — anchoring the jewel box to his saddle and pressing downwards on it with his doubled left elbow — then, sitting awkwardly, he fetched his mount around in mid-street and spurred off westwards, reckoning that whatever the peculiarity of any possible development here in town, no pursuit would get started within the next thirty minutes.

Going plenty fast enough, Hawkins cleared Rock Springs and, guessing at his position thereafter — since he could not see much by the flickering starlight — left the trail about a quarter of a mile out and set off across the land, slowing before long and then feeling his way back to the climb which led up to the ridge that was surmounted by the jaws of stone. With the rocky narrows negotiated, he rode down the reverse side of the ascent and along the floor of the valley beyond, his eyes fully accustomed to the darkness of the lower ground by now and able to pick out enough of the spectral details in the background to locate the position of the waterhole that was ringed by trees and that also of the shack not far ahead and to its right.

He rode up to the tiny building's front door. Here he stopped his horse and dismounted. Then, with the jewel box tucked under his left arm, he pushed open the door of the shack and ducked inside, a cheery word springing readily to his lips as he glanced around him in the absolute blackness of the shanty's small room. But all speech in him was stillborn, for the atmosphere was thick with the stench of burned lamp oil and, knowing that the odour should not be present, he gave a startled gasp and made a move towards his gun.

In the same instant what appeared to be a covering oilskin was whipped off an already lighted lantern and Hawkins blinked at the brightness of the glow, only half seeing the figures that moved in his vicinity during the following seconds in which he was purblind. Then a hand that was operating faster than his own relieved him of his Colt, while a buffeting shoulder knocked him sufficiently off balance to prevent him making any other offensive movement for now.

"Well done, Alec!" Horace Lemon's voice approved from the further end of the shack, where the big man's person came into focus for Hawkins as something of a leering ogre with Ellen Copperstone standing pale and mute within his clasp, her injured foot raised and balanced lightly on its toes. "As for you, Hawkins, it looks to me as if you've been a busy man and that your industry could have served me well tonight. That box if you please — or even if you don't!"

Alec Ford stretched out his hands peremptorily, and Hawkins put the box which contained the jewels into them. After that he stood glumly silent, for what had obviously happened here in his absence was a possibility that he should not have overlooked for a moment — let alone completely!

8

HAWKINS watched Alec Ford open first the outer box and then the inner one in which the jewels were actually encased. Ford was holding his gun very awkwardly while he did all this, and it would not have been hard to pounce on him had his been the only weapon bared, but in fact the two other hardcases in Horace Lemon's employ — Thomson and the somewhat smaller tough guy whose name Hawkins had yet to hear — were standing well back into the corner near the pot-bellied stove and covering him with the muzzles of their pistols through every moment of the time. Now everybody stirred excitedly as Ford emitted a loud chortle and drew out the tiara, which Hawkins had earlier recognised as the box's star piece, for all present to see. "Night at the opera, Horace?" Ford wondered, the slit of a half raised eye mocking. "It's no fair world, is it, sir? One poor bitch slogs at the washtub and wipes snotty noses, while another struts a red carpet with a crown worth a fortune on her head." He spat dryly from the corner of his mouth. "No, it sure ain't a fair world!"

"When did you start to care about that, Alec?" Lemon demanded, treating Hawkins to a sneer by proxy. "I see ten thousand dollars in your hand — and some of it is yours."

"But very little, I think," Ford mused.

"Hey, hey!" Lemon protested, calling his subordinate to order. "By rights it should all be mine."

"If you say so," Ford replied, his lean face appearing momentarily wolfish.

"You agreed to the rate of pay when you took on the job," Lemon reminded. "You were satisfied then. I hope you haven't ceased to be."

"No," Ford said flatly. "When I

make a bargain, I stick to it — more or less."

"Then let it be more, young man," Lemon encouraged, the spiky hair around his bald crown seeming to stand erect as the pallid skin of the tonsure glutted redly. "I may yet pay a bonus. What would you say to that, Thomson and Dunbar?"

The two gunmen dominating the room from the corner behind the stove murmured their approval, jiggling at the hammers of their six-shooters, and Ford raised his chin sharply and gazed at them narrowly.

"Greed is one of the deadly sins," Lemon pursued, clearly feeling that the younger man had taken his point.

"You would know, Horace," Ford commented stonily. "Mary Copperstone was your wife. She should have known better where to will the goodies. It's been tricky. But — all's well that ends well. Yeah?"

"Indeed," Lemon agreed. "You look sick at heart, Hawkins."

"At my stomach, maybe," Hawkins corrected. "It comes of looking at you."

"Does it now?" Lemon said, sounding pained. "Punish him, Alec!"

Ford thumped a fist into Hawkins' solar plexus, but there was less force behind the punch than there might have been; and, expecting something of the sort, he merely gasped and doubled slightly forward, absorbing the blow with tensed muscles and feeling no real hurt. "Thanks, pal!" he wheezed.

"You're a cheeky hellion, Hawkins!" Ford declared, grinning faintly despite himself. "I wanted to shoot you when we entered this valley and I saw you plodding up that hill yonder. But the boss wouldn't have it. He says he's got something real nice planned for you and Ellen."

"I have," Lemon assured the captives. "I'm going to reward you, for all the trouble you've caused me, with the opportunity to get to know each other about as well as possible — before you eventually die."

"Wasn't something like that Alec Ford's privilege?" Hawkins inquired innocently.

"Don't push it, Sam!" Ford cautioned.

"It's a privilege I've decided to withdraw in his case," Lemon said arrogantly. "Alec missed his chance this afternoon. And he's been getting above himself. Besides, I want all this mayhem and trudging around the countryside ended as swiftly as possible now. Rock Springs is a sordid little town, and I wish to shake its dust off my feet."

"How's that to come about, master?" Hawkins twitted.

"You won't be so jaunty, my friend," Horace Lemon promised grimly, "when we get to it."

"I'm pretty sure I can guess what you have in mind, Horace," Ford remarked. "But it's too dark outside to do much at present." He considered Ellen with a pair of lustful eyes that made her cower back into the older man's grasp. "You can't deny me that girl, mister — I won't have it! Me and Ellen can

176

work up a real lather between now and sunup, and we won't need much space to do it in."

"Forget it, Alec," Lemon advised. "Since when were you the slave of your loins, man? I have said no, and I mean no. We don't have all night, and I've given you my reason why not, I want this finished. We have a lantern, don't we? I told you it was for seeing in the dark when we helped ourselves to it."

Hawkins was standing close enough to Ford to pick up the vibrations of the other's entire being. There was a switchback of discord present, and Hawkins sensed that the tall man was close to venting a great rage. What he had seen in the jewel box had undoubtedly stirred up his jealousy and greed, and Lemon's foolishly overbearing responses had done nothing to help. It was almost as if some unseen force — perhaps that of fatigue and recent frustration — were trying to stir up trouble here, but Hawkins had no doubt that, while Ford had no fear of

Lemon, he was wary of Thomson and Dunbar and knew that he must hang on to his temper. The man appeared to resign himself to behaving for now, but his hidden demeanour was that of somebody who, while spoiling for trouble — if only as a source of nervous relief — seemed to feel that he would have a better chance of making his presence felt later. "Okay, Horace," he said. "You seem to be telling me a sight too much just lately. But that's jake with me, I guess. You'll be paying for the right presently."

"Now you're talking sensibly again," Lemon responded, sounding relieved. "What a tart, rebellious, wrong-headed young fellow you can be. Thank God I have patience!"

Ford grinned bleakly, as if he were thanking God that he had it too; and then he said: "So what do you want?"

"We go back to the mine — now," Lemon answered. "I'll tell you what I want done when we get there."

"I told you," Ford said — "I can imagine. Are you going to bring the girl along or do you want to carry the box?"

"I'll bring the girl," the older man replied. "You carry the box and keep your gun in Hawkins' back. Frank Dunbar can bring the lantern, and Les Thomson can keep watch over-all."

Ford reached past Hawkins and opened the door of the shack to its widest extent. Horace Lemon initiated the first move towards the night. Holding Ellen Copperstone at the backs of her upper arms, he steered the limping girl over the threshold and stepped outside at her heels. Then the pudgy and booze-reddened Dunbar bent his blunt features to the front and picked up the lantern — a rusty and calcinated object if ever there was one — from besides the bunk, moving out behind the pair after that and providing the light for them to walk by. Now Alec Ford ordered Hawkins to turn around — which Hawkins did, shuffling a bit in the confined space — and then the tall man shoved the muzzle of his Colt against the male prisoner's spine and forced him out into the night. The thick-shouldered Thomson — with his broad-seated nose and dead eyes — brought up the rear, walking almost in darkness as he supervised the short procession that moved ahead of him.

Hawkins carefully matched his strides to those of the people leading the way. He sensed that it would be madness to attempt anything clever just now. The influences of the hour were all against him. But his mind was more occupied by thoughts about the mine which Lemon had mentioned anyway. He felt that, considering the day's orbit, the diggings — though unknown to him — could not be far away, and perhaps only on the other side of the black ridge which they were approaching now. Just as there was plenty about his visit to town which Lemon and company could not know, so there had naturally been things in their day that he was not aware of. Perhaps poking around on that field of rocky chaos beyond the stone wall on his left had revealed more to them than Ellen and he could have dreamed likely when they had passed into the fissure behind the ridge and found their way to the derelict shack in this valley. He was dealing with the obvious, perhaps, but the facts could not be ignored.

Now the light from the lantern shone directly on the rearing wall that blocked off immediate access to the south, and the entrance to the great crack that sectioned off the defile along its back became visible on the left. Entering the rift, they walked without much change of pace to its further end and passed out onto the floor of the largely open space which formed the big semi-circle of ruin beyond. Horace Lemon's actual movements provided the only directions for the people following him but, regardless of the night's many confusing obscurities, he appeared to know exactly where he was going, and presently the party entered what Hawkins judged to be the southwest semi-arc of the rocky space. Here, after skirting a bed of rubble and detritus, they came to a heap of small boulders which seemed to have significance for Lemon and his hirelings. For the men halted in front of the pile and Dunbar began casting around with the lantern as he hunted for something that had to be lying nearby and was perhaps of marginal danger to those present.

It seemed that suddenly Dunbar met with success, for he grunted loudly with satisfaction, and he set his lantern down beside a square hole in the floor of the place that Hawkins instantly recognised as an adit or the vertical entrance to a mine that had been driven straight down into the earth as opposed to the more usual method of cutting horizontally into rock where veins of precious metal were suspected. "There you are, suh," Dunbar said to Lemon. "There's your hole in the floor. Though whatever of any worth a sourdough hoped to take out of a place like this will remain a licker to me."

"Ditto," Lemon confessed. "Yes, we may suppose that whoever dug this hole found it pretty unrewarding. But we can take benefit from it. There was never a better grave than this. If we bury my sister-in-law and Sam Hawkins in it, they'll lie undiscovered until the Last Trumpet sounds. Nobody is going to look down there for them."

"That's what I figured," Alec Ford sniffed. "You're going to bury them alive."

"Do you object?" Lemon queried, sounding a little dangerous again.

"Hell, no!" Ford responded. "Get on with it."

"You get on with it," Lemon ordered.

"Sure thing," Ford said. "There can't be a whole lot to it, can there? Whoever dug the mine left his ladder in place. Climb down there, Hawkins. You, too, Ellen. It's only about a dozen feet."

Hawkins was scared and angry, but

also cold inside. There was a feeling of inevitability present that he did not seem to have the will or strength of spirit to challenge. Doubtless he could talk up a delay, but this was going to happen whatever he did. He felt past quarrelling with Fortune; so, going to the adit, he leaned sideways and put a boot down into it, feeling around until he located the ladder. Then, settling a sole onto an upper rung, he lowered himself into the hole and began climbing downwards, coming to the bottom of the mine a moment or so later. Now he stepped back and gazed upwards. Some of the light from the lantern above reached him — and he received the impression of brief, tomblike spaces about him — but then the glow was almost completely cut out as Ellen entered the aperture above and started her descent. For brief seconds the ladder vibrated audibly, and then the girl stepped off the homemade climbing aid and joined him, looking up as he looked upwards likewise.

There were faint noises around the top of the trap. Then a shadowy figure crouched over the adit. Next the lantern itself was lowered to arm's-length into the mine, and Lemon's face became visible above the light. "Are you snug, Ellen?" he inquired. "I'm leaving you to die, my dear, but you'll have a companion for consolation. I'd like to leave you the lantern too — since we found it hanging down there — but I have need of it myself. I promise to think of you occasionally, while I'm delving into the fleshpots of the Barbary Coast, and I'll raise a champagne glass to you every time I sell a trinket." He chuckled deep in his throat, echoes of his sinister merriment dully circulating the walls of the mine. "When you reach heaven, Ellen, give my regards to your sister Mary. I know she tried to be a good wife, but she had no talent for the married state. Ask her about those pains which preceded her death. Could they have been arsenical? She wondered then, but she'll know now."

"You fiend!" Ellen cried. "You murdered her!"

"Did I so?" Lemon queried. "Well, perhaps, dear Ellen. Yesterday's troubles, eh? I bid you farewell — !"

A gun went off above and behind the man hanging down through the adit. It seemed to Hawkins that Lemon's face turned to stone, as his head, shot through from back to front, suddenly burst open at the left temple and poured out a brief flood of blood and brains. After that, dripping heavily, the big man just hung there, chin propped by a rung of the ladder, and the lantern slipped out of the slowly opening fingers of his left hand and fell to the floor beneath, where amazingly enough, it landed on its base plate and just stood there, burning still.

"All right, Alec!" Hawkins shouted up comprehendingly. "I figure you've done what you always intended to do and killed Horace Lemon. You've got the jewels, and Ellen Copperstone is down here for the taking. So take her."

"I've got problems enough," came Ford's retort. "I'm not so sure I want her any more."

"Yes, you do," Hawkins assured him. "Mostly because you've got one problem more than you think."

"Oh, what's that?"

"You've got the jewels," Hawkins responded, doing all in his power to guide the other's mind for the girl's sake, "but you haven't got the savvy to get shut of them at a profit. Ellen has. Those stones belong to her class, not ours, boy."

"What're you talking about, dopey?" Ford scorned. "Have you forgotten that German guy already? He can sell them as readily for me as he could Ellen. Don't try to faze me, feller; I know what you're on. And you make me sick!"

"Alec," Hawkins said evenly, "Adolf Kline isn't there any more. Jason Wellard killed Kline this evening and stole the jewels from the old guy's safe. I got them back off Wellard."

"You telling me the truth, Sam?" Ford rasped.

"Honour bright."

"God-dammit!" blasphemed the unseen man above, adding a further curse or two of the more sulphurous kind. "I reckon you killed Wellard."

"No," Hawkins said. "He got away on horseback. Going eastwards."

"Never did trust the long son-of-a-bitch!" Alec Ford declared. "But him and Horace Lemon got on. Birds of a feather, I guess."

"Sure as fate!"

"Will he come back?"

"You must find your own answer to that."

"Yeah." Ford was undoubtedly musing. "You'll do anything to get Ellen saved, won't you? Fact is, you're right about that other thing too. I do have need of her. I don't know a diamond from a collar stud." He paused, possibly seeking an extra cruel effect to soothe his underlying anger. "What about you, Sam?"

"What about me?" Hawkins asked tersely. "I know I'm done for."

"Why don't you beg, Sam?"

"Like hell, Alec!"

"You know me okay," Ford agreed; and then the body hanging into the mine began to slide downwards — presumably with the thrust of the speaker's hands behind it — and it finally plunged straight to the floor and lay there as limp and empty as a newly killed beast in the shambles. "Ellen, come on up!"

The girl swung on Hawkins, pain in her face. "Sam — " she began.

"Forget all that!" Hawkins interrupted emphatically. "Not a word about me — not a word about anything! Just run up that ladder — right now!"

"Sam, please!"

"Go!" he insisted.

She went, face crumpling. Hawkins felt a great relief as he watched her clamber out of the mine. To be buried alive was among the worst fates that could befall any man, and it was one that no woman should ever be called upon to suffer. Rape must be a sickening experience; but, as he saw it, any amount of violation was better than being entombed alive.

Now the girl was out of the mine and clear of the adit. Hawkins heard Ford speak again, though not to him. "Block that hole up, boys," he ordered, obviously addressing Les Thomson and Frank Dunbar. "Use the heaviest lump of rock you can manage. And make sure it fits right. This world must never hear another peep out of him. Hurry it, hey?"

"The light's down there," a voice which sounded like Frank Dunbar's reminded.

"So what?" Ford demanded irritably. "I'd give you a hand, dammit, but I've got to watch this girl. We can't have her running off!"

Hawkins expected the closing of his grave to take time, but it didn't. Thomson and Dunbar fetched a piece of rock to the adit almost straightaway and sealed him in. He stood there, arms akimbo, and the light from the lantern rose up into the mine's airless gloom and played on the dark underside of the rock that now cut him off from the night. It was done; he was a prisoner of the sepulchre. Two days of increasing torture lay ahead, then thirst would kill him. But was that the worst of it? He gazed around him tensely. In fact he was standing in a crude excavation of no more than eight by six. Sure, there was the depth of the place too; but, when you came to multiply it all up — and worked out the amount of breathable air present — he was going to stifle before too many hours had gone by. Now the panic hit him, and he reeled against the wall and shook and sweated, hiding his face. This could hardly be worse, and there was no possible way out.

9

HAWKINS made a huge effort and pulled himself together. When an evil thing happened to you in life, it only became worse if you lost your nerve. Nor had he ever known a situation so bad that there wasn't also some good in it, if you sought hard enough to find it. He would make an exercise of this one before long and do a bit of seeking; but first he must climb the ladder and check that stone up there, for it might not be as immovable as it looked.

Knowing that, just as a man could despair too much he could also let himself grow too optimistic, Hawkins made his ascent, and then he raised his hands and put all the power of his body into trying to move the rock that sealed the adit. The stone — though deeply cracked and old on its underside — did not shift by the tiniest fraction of an inch, and he realized that he would need to be far stronger than in fact he was to force his way out of this tomb by muscle-power alone.

Not too depressed — since he had already accepted that he was totally trapped — Hawkins returned to the floor of the mine and sat down with his back against the bottom of the ladder, bowing his head in thought. He had at least been left with the lantern, and that could so easily have been otherwise. How long the light would burn, he did not particularly wish to find out — for the flame was going to keep robbing him of some of the precious oxygen in here — but, on the other hand, the presence of the light itself meant a very great deal, so he did have a basic curiosity concerning it that would not be denied.

If, as Horace Lemon had said, the lantern had originally been taken from this mine — and there was indeed a wall bracket at the back of the place from which it could have hung — it had almost certainly possessed a full reservoir of oil to start with. Had it been otherwise, the process of evaporation would probably have emptied it long ago — always taking it for granted that the diggings had not been worked in years — so he reckoned that he could make his calculation on the basis of a full reservoir of oil providing light for around twelve hours. Assuming the light had already been burning for about a quarter of that time, he could expect the lantern flame to endure for perhaps eight hours more. All this was being figured on the roughest lines, of course, but he and the lantern would probably last around the same length of time. Well, whatever happened, his end was still a fair way off, and he could do a lot of thinking and suffering between now and then.

Hawkins felt that the greatest drawback in his situation was the nearby presence of Horace Lemon's body. But then he realized that something very important which had to do with the corpse had escaped him until that moment. Grisly company the dead and bloody Lemon might be, but his clothing was still clean enough and his pockets were there to be emptied whenever the man sharing the floor with him wished it. A fellow of education and some means, the late Horace Lemon could well be carrying objects of special worth in a situation like this. It was only right to find out.

Suppressing all feelings of distaste, Hawkins rose to his feet at once and went to the dead man. Bending over the corpse, he rifled through the pockets of Lemon's jacket and trousers, taking from them and laying aside a hip flask, empty, a cigar case, full, a wallet holding a sum of paper money, a pocket-knife, some change, and a handkerchief. Additionally, there was a thirty-eight calibre Smith and Wesson revolver which nestled in a deep inside pocket with two boxes of ammunition, each still sealed and holding two dozen cartridges.

Hawkins sighed and shook his head. There was nothing special here. These were objects that might be found on any man. What had he been expecting anyway? He really could not explain the vague disappointment which filled him as he picked the items over a second and third time. Perhaps his desperation was sending out a plea to some Superior Power for a magical delivery. If so, he had been around long enough to know that he had little chance of being answered. Yet in the same moment he was filled with an inner illumination that made him gasp aloud at his own previous obtuseness. There could still be a way out of this! It would be a one and only chance, and he would have to get it exactly right — allowing that it would work at all — but there was definitely an outside possibility here that he could still extricate himself from what continued to look like a position of certain death.

He spread out Horace Lemon's handkerchief on the floor. After that he opened the small blade of the dead man's pocket-knife. Next he broke the seal on one of the boxes of pistol ammunition and tipped out the shells the box contained. Then, working faster than was safe or comfortable — for the matter of the light's perhaps uncertain duration was suddenly far more important than before — he picked up and prised open one of the cartridges, throwing aside its leaden slug and tipping out its charge of explosive powder onto the handkerchief. With the first bullet broken open and emptied, he did the same to a second and a third — moving on to do the same with all the shells from the first box and building a heap of dark powder at the middle of the handkerchief — and, having gone that far, he opened the second box and did the same all over again, his cut fingers shaking and the pressure of his blood singing in his ears. Then, with the second box as fully plundered as the first — and the metallic remains cast aside — he opened Lemon's gun and tipped out the bullets from its cylinder, soon adding the powder from the cases to that which now made a considerable heap on Lemon's handkerchief.

Hawkins rested just long enough to draw three deep breaths and clear his head. Then he spread the propellant from the cartridges across the centre of the linen square and rolled it up into a sausage-shape within the material. After that, with his floppy cylinder twisted up at either end and held out horizontally between his hands, he returned to the ladder and started climbing it again, while guiding himself upwards by the pressure of his forearms against the ladder's staves. At the top of his ascent, he ducked beneath the stone that covered the adit above him and considered the cracks present in its base, employing the utmost care as he eased the cloth cylinder containing the explosive powder into the longest and deepest of these. Now he gently poked and prodded at the powder-filled shape, making it fit the crack in which it rested as perfectly as possible and, when all was done to his satisfaction, he began descending to the floor again — fearful as he put pressure on each rung in turn that the vibrations of his movements would cause the sausage-shape to come out of its housing and fall to the floor, scattering the explosive material all over the place and rendering it of no further use to him.

No such disaster occurred, however, and, leaving the foot of the ladder, Hawkins stepped up to Horace Lemon's body anew and tipped it onto its back. Now he removed the string cravat from the deceased's soft collar and stretched it out and smoothed it between his hands. After that he went to the lantern and, kneeling before it, took out the reservoir plug and exposed the paraffin left inside it. Again working with extreme care, Hawkins fed the string cravat into the little oil tank and soaked the material from one end to the other, withdrawing it into the cupped palm of his right hand and holding it with almost no squeezing pressure from his fingers at all.

Coming erect once more, he moved to the ladder yet again. Up the rungs he climbed, still treading lightly and suppressing the great excitement which now filled him. Reaching the limit of his ascent again, he stopped and forced himself to get total control of his entire body before lifting his hands to the explosive charge which he had recently set in place. Now he slowly untwisted the linen at the nearer end of the sausage-shape and made a hole in the explosive granules beyond with the tip of his little finger. Inserting an oil-soaked inch of the cravat into the terminal part of his miniature mine, Hawkins screwed up the linen end of the sausage-shape with a newly learned dexterity and extended the rest of the cravat down the front of the rungs before him so that its weight was borne by the ladder itself.

Hawkins moved back in the direction of the floor again, gazing upwards as he did so. Everything was in place and appeared capable of creating the explosion he intended. There was, of course, the danger that, when lighted, the flame running up his fuse would increase the weight of the oil-soaked material with its movement and pull the cravat out of the explosive and cause it to fall. If that happened — He could not be worse off than he had been at the outset. But if all went well and the explosion occurred, it should prove strong enough to split the stone that was imprisoning him. That was the hope upon which he had to concentrate.

Suddenly fearful in the highest degree, despite all, Hawkins thrust a hand into a trouser-pocket and extracted a match, holding it up before him with a thumbnail poised to flick and strike, but somehow he could not quite bring himself to it and stood there for a long moment, considering all and nothing for about the twelfth time; but then a quivering in the lantern's wick reminded him of how much of the light's paraffin he had just soaked up in order to fashion his makeshift fuse and he realized that he was under more pressure than he had imagined to get this done before the lantern went out and he was left in the dark.

He drew the deepest breath he could; then, holding the air in his lungs, he put his flame to the oil-impregnated cravat and the fire instantly took hold and began running up the string necktie. The paraffin was, of course, among the most swiftly combustible of the lamp oils, and it came home to Hawkins very abruptly, as the flame in his fuse twisted and darted upwards, that he was standing right in the path of whatever down-blast might result from the detonation of the powder above, and he dived quickly to his left and crouched into the front corner of the diggings on that side, hiding his face in the angle of the stone there and covering his ears with his hands. He held himself steady, quivering inwardly for all that. One, two, three, four — Must he count interminably? Then a dull, rending boom filled the space around him, and the mine appeared to rock, while its previously stuffy atmosphere seemed to become almost instantly unbreathable.

Retching and choking, Hawkins turned out of his corner and flew back to the ladder. His movements were panic-stricken, for it occurred to him that the climbing aid was almost bound to have been damaged, if not shattered, by the blast; but in fact he found it still in place and, it seemed to him, as he reached upwards with his fingertips, that the staves and rungs were still whole from its top to bottom. Up it he went, eyes shut and breath held in check and, striking his crown at the limit of the ascent, experienced a dismay that more than matched his pain, since it seemed that the explosion — while it had achieved the force that he had thought necessary — had not sufficiently damaged the adit's seal to either let him shove the remains aside or break up what was left.

Hunched upon the ladder, Hawkins kept denying his need to breathe; but the moment came when he could no longer hold his need for air in check and a polluted inhalation rolled down his gulping throat and filled his chest. He began to cough and gasp almost uncontrollably. Yet, uncomfortable though this tainted respiration was, he found that he was not entirely overcome by the choking process and that his second breath was much less stifling than the first, while the third was not bad at all; and he realized then that the explosion must have achieved at least part of what had been required of it and that he had obviously opened up a vent of sorts and would now be getting a supply of fresh air into the mine for as long as he needed it. But he found the meaning of that phrase hardly less ominous than it would have sounded in his previous circumstances; for, assuming that he was still trapped down here, the ability to keep on breathing indefinitely would do little more than lengthen his sufferings from thirst. Yes, he might be able to yell for help — with some chance of being heard outside — but who would be around up there to hear him? For he doubted if the godforsaken ground above him was visited more than once a year by man or child.

The air soon cleared considerably around Hawkins' head and, looking down through the dust that floated beneath him, he saw that the lantern was still burning and giving off about the same glow as before. There was enough light anyhow to let him closely inspect the cracked rock that he had just now blasted. The stone was black with soot and stank of nitrates, and the crack into which the explosives had been packed was torn open, but there was little evidence visible that any real damage had been done to the seal. It was not until Hawkins placed both palms against the rock and gave it a kind of exasperated push that the right-hand corner of the stone broke away and he felt a draught upon his face that was obviously drawing straight in from the night.

He breathed more freely. It was success of a sort, but nothing to get excited about, and Hawkins simply thrust a hand through the hole that he had made, hoping to feel his way above the larger mass of the rock which still covered him and perhaps pass his fingertips over its top. When all was said and done, the entire stone had been lifted into place by two men and could not be that huge. But this movement — vague in purpose to say the least of it — had hardly begun, when another and far more substantial chunk of stone broke away from the greater mass and left a hole through which he could see a number of stars in a circle of sky directly above him.

He thought about it anew. There could be no harm in repeating what he had just done on a larger scale and, gripping the rough edges of stone which he had just bared, Hawkins tensed his muscles and set himself to attempt shaking still more of the rock adrift. He hardly believed for an instant that he would meet with further success, so he was amazed and delighted when, as he brought his full strength to bear, the remaining piece of rock moved in a manner which told him that it was broken through its centre and no longer an impossible stopper. Shifting his position a little to the left on the ladder beneath him, he got the best of his muscle under the portion of the seal closest to him and thrust upwards and turned the mass aside, clearing a space large enough to admit his head and shoulders to the open. Then, first bringing up his arms, he slowly climbed the rest of the ladder and put down his hands at either side of the adit to help force him the rest of the way out of the diggings. Now he stood once more under the night sky and was tasting the sweetness of airs that seemed permeated by mountain snow and the high forests. It was done. "Thank God for that," he said simply but sincerely; because he had been a very scared man down there in the mine.

Standing erect, Hawkins allowed his mind and body time to fully recover. Life and purpose had been handed back to him, yes, but everything still seemed just out of drawing. His problems had not changed, but he must come to grips with them anew. The prospect of dying had taken away his sense of responsibility, and it was hard to pick up again. He might just have risen from the earth reborn. Those newly come into the world had no past. All he had to do was walk away from this spot and start afresh. Nobody would know, and few would care. He could begin writing on a clean sheet and perhaps fashion his life into a new and better story. If only it could really be that easy. But he knew that Sam Hawkins would not let Sam Hawkins get away with that. This version of the yarn had to be fully told. If the present page still left him dead, then so be it. If he could face Eternity knowing that he had skimped nothing that was his to do, he would rest content. But, heck now, these were mighty peculiar thoughts for a guy like him — regardless of what he might just have gone through!

He forced his mind to square up to its problems. First and foremost, he asked himself where Alec Ford would most likely have led his little party after they had left him, Hawkins, sealed into the mine. He had, of course, no means of knowing, yet felt that it could not be far. Ellen Copperstone's sprained ankle would to some extent limit the party's movement. True, Alec Ford would not give a cuss for Ellen's suffering — and force left a prisoner no room for argument — but a person afflicted with a bad injury of the kind could only walk so far before collapsing. He, Hawkins, had made the best sort of job he could of strapping up Ellen's ankle — and she had certainly walked on it almost normally while Horace Lemon had been holding her from the rear — but even so her mobility would have to be rather limited and Ford would need to get her onto horseback before he could hope to take her very far.

Leaving the adit from which he had recently escaped, and thinking hard as he went along, Hawkins walked slowly back in the direction of the shack beyond the rock wall to the north of him. He had left his horse outside the little building and wondered if Ford could have gone back there, with the intention of appropriating the mount for Ellen's use — which seemed a logical enough thing to do — yet he had the feeling that Ford would have been thinking more in terms of getting all his people mounted rather than the girl only and might well have not retraced his steps in this direction at all. It went without saying that Ford and the two hardcases in his company had mounts awaiting them in Rock Springs and that a horse could be obtained there for Ellen without too much difficulty; so the probability was that Ford would have taken his party some distance afield after leaving Hawkins entombed, made camp at a convenient spot, then sent Les Thomson and Frank Dunbar into town to solve the horse problem for him. That would have been a long while ago — for Hawkins judged that the hour must be well after midnight now and not too far short of sunup — and the two hardcases could easily have returned to their sender by this time and whatever journey Ford had planned for the immediate future even got started.

But Hawkins couldn't really see it like that. The basic human elements always had to be taken into account.

There were tired people involved, and Dunbar and Thomson were well aware that Ford had designs on Ellen Copperstone. It figured that, whether asked or otherwise, they would have taken their time while the tall man was pleasuring himself with the girl, which meant that the party was still almost certainly within a mile or two of here and had perhaps decided to rest up until dawn. It was up to him to locate those varmints, rescue Ellen and her very valuable property, and either kill or chase off the men who had her in their power just now. It was a tall order — and he had little idea of how he was to tackle any of it — yet he was confident that it could be done and that he was going to do it.

The night was still extremely dark, and the glitter of the stars didn't reveal many details of the surrounding terrain; but, after much careful groping — not to mention backtracking and more false starts — Hawkins found his way back into the next valley and once again approached the derelict shack. His horse was indeed still waiting for him there, and it greeted him with a soft nicker. Walking up to the animal, he fondled its head rather absently, for his mind was still elsewhere and straining after any special pointers that he might have missed. But his reasoning had been exhaustive and none was to be found. There seemed nothing for it but to mount up and ride off into the darkness on spec. Then everything changed, for a rifle shot split the night with the cracking roll of its blast and Hawkins knew deep within himself that the detonation was the indicator that he had so badly needed.

The explosion had come off the country which lay between him and town. Swinging into leather, he spurred off in the direction of Rock Springs.

10

HAWKINS did not ride at much of a pace for very long. In fact he reined back to no better than a walk while climbing his mount out of the valley. He knew from experience that even the sound of a trotting horse could be heard over a fair spread of land, and he could not be sure just how far away the individual who had recently fired the shot might be. He had had his share of luck tonight and did not wish to throw dirt in the Lady's face by riding straight up the barrel of a hostile rifle.

Again he topped out, and once more he passed through the jaws of rock that occupied the summit. Reaching the edge of the reverse slope, he gazed into the black distance beyond. There, forming gapped chains and dull clusters, the night lights of Rock

Springs seemed to float in space; yet, checking as his heart quickened, he found himself less interested in this display than in the single rose of fire that glowed against the lower ground perhaps three-quarters of a mile to his right. Easing his mount's head round, he made for the tiny blotch of scarlet, riding the shoulder of the incline that he could sense toppling away from him on his left. The urge was strong in him to find out what had happened yonder, but he remained patient and headed for the rose of fire at the same slow pace, though with every nerve tightening to full torsion as he neared the glow and saw that it was the campfire that he had imagined it to be all along and that there was a man lying back in a kind of natural seat formed by the angle of the terraced ground adjacent.

While the light from the fire was not strong enough to fully show the other's face, Hawkins could see that the man was not moving and did not appear to be in the least dangerous.

When he judged himself close enough, Hawkins halted his horse and silently dismounted, flitting away to his left as his soles touched the grass and then moving in on the man at the edge of the firelight from the rear. He did this in order to hold a position that the other would not be able to instantly cover by whipping out his gun — one, also, from which it became any threat to him — but nothing abrupt or desperate occurred and he sensed more and more certainly that the figure before him was either dead or unconscious.

Risking it, he faced round and dropped to his knees at the other's left elbow. Then he caught the fellow's chin in a pinch-grip and raised it, turning the face to which it belonged into the fire's ruddy glow and revealing the features of Alec Ford. A hair stirred in Ford's left nostril. The man was not dead, but a closer examination showed that he had been shot near the centre of the chest and could not have much longer to go. Just then he kicked out his legs and groaned, opening his eyes and peering at Hawkins with a foggy gaze into which comprehension returned but slowly. "You," he muttered.

"Me," Hawkins agreed inconsequentially.

"Am I dead, Sam?"

"Not quite."

"But you must be."

"I'm in a sight better case than you, feller."

"How?"

"Too long a story, Alec. We don't have time for it."

"The devil sure looks after his own!"

Hawkins grinned bleakly at the effort which the exclamation mark had cost the dying man. "Well, pal, you'll soon be in a position to ask him about it."

"Hot damn!"

"That's what they call it round back of the stokehole."

"You're a rat!"

"Some such," Hawkins acknowledged cheerfully. "Did Wellard shoot you?"

"Yeah."

"He took Ellen?"

"And those jewels."

"Figures," Hawkins sighed. "I daresay he never really lost his taste for the girl."

"Some woman!"

"It's never wise to let a women take your mind off staying alive," Hawkins chided. "Thomson and Dunbar gone to town?"

"Seems the skunks met Jason on the way back here. They've thrown in with him."

"Men of their cut will always join up with the party who promises most."

"Promise is the word," Ford reflected, clutching at the air with fingers that could hold nothing. "Jason Wellard is the worst scheming polecat of all."

"You'd know, Alec."

"Blow his cotton-pickin' skull off, Sam!"

"If and when I find him," Hawkins responded. "He won't be going back to Rock Springs. Not if he values his

neck, he won't, murdering bastard!"
He paused reflectively. "Were Thomson
and Dunbar going to bring horses back
here?"

"You know it."

Hawkins nodded. "It means Wellard
is set up to go any direction the
compass points."

"Sure, but he ain't got the — the — "
Ford's voice was suddenly petering out
— "ass for it."

"Alec!" Hawkins shook the man quite
hard, but nothing issued from his throat
save a final sighing breath. "Alec!"

But Ford was gone.

"What were you trying to tell me?"
Hawkins inquired of the dead man,
jacking himself upright and placing his
arms akimbo as he gazed down on
Ford's setting face. "He's not saddle-
hardened, eh? And he's aiming to use
the ironroad? Well, it runs past Rock
Springs, and that's a fact. The good
ole U.P. Des Moines to Sacramento,
and back again. East to west — and
west to east."

Hawkins reached down. He helped himself to the deceased's revolver. Breaking out the loading gate, he checked the pistol's cylinder against the firelight and found its chambers to be carrying the normal load of five cartridges — with an empty space under the hammer — favoured by all men who spent their days heeled. Dropping the Colt into his holster, Hawkins sent his frowning gaze through the night towards the area in which he believed the Rock Springs railroad depot to stand at the town's eastern end. Assuming Wellard did use the Union Pacific to escape from this place, he would be unlikely to appear on the cinder track much before the arrival time of the train he planned to use, and that all too obviously posed the question of whether he would be travelling towards the Atlantic or Pacific coast, since different trains would be involved and their timings also different.

It was a bigger problem than it seemed at first, and it exercised

Hawkins' mind quite considerably, for there were aspects present that played upon the understanding in the deepest fashion. He was far from certain that a man raised as a gentleman, with his roots in America's old world — and perhaps forced by circumstances to uproot when he had not wished it — would continue travelling westwards into an unfamiliar way of life. Nor would it be long before Wellard was on the nation's Wanted list, and that would further dispose him towards the natural conservatism of his upbringing. He would surely find it much easier to lose his present identity in the denser and more civilised population of the Atlantic seaboard. The Pacific coast, on the other hand, was far more thinly peopled and had a much rawer way of life. Because of that it was zealously policed by the marshals of the new Federal Law. In other words, Wellard would stand a much stronger chance of being taken in California than in the Old States, where the law was altogether more urbane and less persistent. Also, when closely thought about — now that Horace Lemon was dead and gone — the selling of Ellen's jewellery should be an easier and more rewarding task among the generally honest jewel traders of the East, for the majority of the country's crooked dealers had already taken up residence in the cities of the West. So, gambling on no more than these salient factors, it appeared to Hawkins that Wellard, needing to get out of Rock Springs before the bereaved Winifred Kline could identify him to the law as her husband's killer, would be aboard the first eastbound train of the day, perhaps wearing some kind of disguise and abandoning all else but Ellen Copperstone and her jewels.

What time did the first eastbound train run? Hawkins was not certain but, during his waggon train's stopover in Rock Springs of a few days ago, he remembered having heard a train out of the west stop at the depot around seven a.m. or the breakfast hour, as you preferred. So far as he was aware, the Union Pacific's transcontinental services were fairly infrequent and ran only about three trains a day in either direction, which meant that the next eastbound train after the one at breakfastime wouldn't halt in Rock Springs before the afternoon, though one or two more would come through from the opposite direction to balance out the long distance service and make it in all senses viable. Altogether, he reckoned that he would do well to ride round the nearby outskirts of town until he reached the railroad depot right now — thus covering all possible services running at the start of the day — and hang on there as long as the situation demanded. If it should prove that his reasoning was all wrong — and Jason Wellard and party did leave the district on horseback — he would just have to ask questions about town until he learned the direction in which the man had gone. There would be nothing for it but to accept the loss of a day and whatever that might ultimately mean; for, while he was sure of his ability to ride down Wellard and company at the last, the question of wasted time could not be ignored. There were waggons now travelling the Californian Trail that needed his presence, for he couldn't expect Ray Mostegg and Joe Sinclair to bear the full responsibility for the Western Marriage Agency of St Louis's brides-to-be indefinitely. Good fellows though Mostegg and Sinclair might be, they were going to become mighty disgruntled if he spent too much time away from the waggon train in circumstances which they could not even guess at. He knew people, and even the best did not like to feel that they were being used. After all, the loss of Ellen Copperstone would not mean too much to them — for all the Agency's rules.

Alec Ford's hat lay beside its dead owner. Hawkins picked the Stetson up and placed it over the deceased's inert features. Then he walked back to his horse and remounted. Kicking the animal into a trot, he gazed eastwards, watching as the glimmer of the false dawn climbed into the heavens there like ghost lightning. The pulsing glow trembled faintly for a minute or two, then snuffed out again, and the land seemed darker than before and the disconnected lighting of Rock Springs floated anew in the blackness under the northern stars. Now a wind sprang up, blustering fitfully like most such winds of the hour, and Hawkins shivered as it infiltrated his garments and chilled his flesh, but otherwise the night was still and seemed to isolate any sound that was not his own.

Hawkins' ride proved better judged than he had feared it might be. He soon came upon the succession of flats and deep cuttings which carried the ironroad. Drawing left, he followed the route across the blowing east and made for the oblong of light, not a mile ahead, which he felt sure could only be the Union Pacific's depot at Rock Springs. This proved the case, and the puffing of a loco in a siding — along with the signal lights burning at the loop points — helped him place the railroad's buildings and the cinder track itself nearby and to the left.

There was a thicket which sprawled down off an embankment. Hawkins turned in behind the growth and stopped his horse. He tied the brute where scrub willow branched thinly, then stepped between the rails and followed them into the station, where he sat down on the buffers near a siding at the depot's eastern end and judged — by casting a narrow glance through the pools of lamplight strung out nearby — that he would have almost all the cinder track in view as the day returned. After that he folded his arms and again summoned up his patience, the determination to hold firm once more strong in him.

After a time he probably dozed a little. For there was a period when an atmosphere of disquiet seemed to fill his inner being. Then he was suddenly aware that the world was grey and misty about him and that shapes had their familiar looks and places upon it. There were men around too — railroad workers who took little notice of him — and the smells of coffee and tobacco smoke issued from the nearby staff canteen. Somewhere up the line an engine began shunting box cars, steamy smoke rising darkly and steel couplings on the clang and rattle, and the vapours drawn from the earth by the rising sun hovered at the edges of the scene and thinned. Hawkins yawned, and the minutes dragged by, the time seeming interminable. Chilled to the bone, he wondered confusedly why he had been so stubbornly set all this while; yet, in a place that did not know him, he did not see how he could have managed things otherwise. He'd been forced to rely entirely on himself.

Then it was full light. A yellow sun stood big on the left, and the morning glowed with dew and freshness. The depot stirred; there was a feeling of gathering anticipation. Hawkins saw goods being carried out of the warehouse for transport, and travellers, variously dressed and encumbered, stepped into view from beneath the depot's awning. A signal dropped on Hawkins' left with a gallows thud, and the points that governed the loop clattered into place and locked squeakily. A train was clearly due, and the watcher reckoned that it could only be the eastbound one on which his original plan of action had been based.

Hawkins rose from his seat on the buffers. Hitching his gunbelt, he walked out onto the eastern end of the cinder track, quickly peering down its length and taking in the faces and shapes of the folk standing there; but no two people who even slightly resembled Jason Wellard and Ellen Copperstone were to be seen. This made him a trifle uneasy, but he was not ready to let it modify his earlier prediction of events as yet; for, if Jason and the girl were lurking around the depot, Wellard would be unlikely to rise exposing Ellen and himself to possible recognition from any quarter at all until the oncoming eastbound train had actually stopped in the station and the passengers planning to board it had coalesced into that kind of jockeying corporate body which swallowed up individual identities for the moment to all but eyes that were seeking most intently.

Hawkins went on peering along the cinder track with a steely fixity. Before long he heard the eastbound train and then saw it approaching. He watched it brake to a panting halt down the station's length, smoke belching upwards from its triangular funnel and steam that reeked of lubricants hissing out of valves and joints all over the place. Movement appeared on the boarding platforms of the passenger cars, and a few people left the train and went crunching about their business over the cinders, while the fair number of individuals wishing to get on moved up to the boarding steps and shuffled impatiently as they waited their turns to climb into the vestibules above. In a minute it was done, and the Union Pacific's latest passengers began dispersing down the length of the train and finding seats. But of Jason Wellard and Ellen Copperstone there was still no sign.

Scowling again, Hawkins vented a harsh sigh to match. He realized that he was still at the mercy of the innumerable permutations of a situation that might not even exist in any form that he had imagined. The advantages of choice were all with the fugitives, and the interplay of those choices could baffle a man as many times as there were. Yet every part of him was willing something to happen, and he felt an irrational annoyance that events did not respond to his promptings. Logic was being offended by it all. He was making a fool of himself in his own eyes.

Then his doubt and frustration ended. There was movement, swift and furtive, down at the further end of the train. Frank Dunbar and Les Thomson had suddenly materialised on the ground near the observation car. The two men, hands close to their holsters, cast rapid glances around them; then, appearing satisfied that there was nobody standing in the vicinity who mattered, Thomson twisted to his left and jerked his chin at somebody as yet unseen on the townward side of the steel tracks. Now Jason Wellard stepped into view from behind one of the U.P. depot's administrative buildings. He held Ellen's jewel box under his left arm, and was directing the girl herself by the grip of his right hand. Giving her a bullying shake, he ordered the young woman to board the train up its rear steps.

Hawkins jerked his revolver. He must not lack decision from this moment onwards. "Hold it right where you are,

Wellard!" he shouted, breaking into a run and heading down the length of the cinder track. Legs scissoring as seldom before, he saw Dunbar and Thomson face round and prepare to draw on him, but he blasted a shot in their direction and they went scuttling into cover like frightened sheep.

Ellen looked round, wide-eyed, and Wellard tried to tighten his grip on her.

"This way," Hawkins yelled — "to me!"

The girl tore herself out of Wellard's grasp. She threw herself in Hawkins' direction, but had not covered more than two yards when the loose material under her soles caused her to slip forward and go sprawling on her face.

Plainly caught in two minds, Wellard essayed a new grab at her but, seeming to realize in the same instant that she was lying too low, backed off and reached inside his coat. It was obvious that he was trying to pull a gun, but he failed to locate the weapon at his first attempt and then appeared to perceive that the oncoming Hawkins would now be on top of him before he could get his firearm into action; so, whirling round in pure desperation, he scooped up a chunk of stone that was lying at the end of a nearby tie.

The find was indeed providential and, with a shout of triumph, Wellard hurled the rock at the charging Hawkins with all his force. The missile fairly hurtled through the air, dead on target, and Hawkins flung up his right hand to protect himself — sure that the rock was going to break his arm at least — but, as luck would have it, it struck his revolver instead of bone and tore the weapon from his fingers, leaving him unhurt if also unarmed.

The rhythm of Hawkins' strides was broken by the impact, and he lurched into a kind of ungainly dancing step which carried him safely above the still sprawling Ellen. After that he staggered over the remaining brief stretch of ground between Wellard and himself, ending up face to face with the man. If a few moments ago Hawkins had seemed to hold the advantage, the situation had now reversed itself, and Wellard brought over a terrific right-hander that literally exploded against the side of his attacker's jaw and Hawkins dropped to his hands and knees where he stood. But, crouching there, with his senses whirling he refused to lose consciousness.

He saw Wellard loose a kick at his head and threw up his arms to fend it off as best he could. Wellard's boot passed beyond the shielding limbs, but his shinbone connected with them and the elasticity created by the contact threw him off balance in his turn and he went staggering backwards into a heavy collision with a corner of the rails that surrounded the observation platform at the end of the train's rear car. He fell to his backside, but was winded rather than hurt, and he beat Hawkins back to the vertical and was in good enough case to send his man reeling and then yell at Thomson and Dunbar to get their guns into action.

Catching himself, Hawkins shook his head to clear his vision. He feared those guns behind him, but realized that he would have no hope of recovering his own fallen weapon — even if he could see where it lay — and figured that his best chance of avoiding a bullet fired from short range must be to keep as close to Wellard as possible, for any shot then fired at him would carry the risk of hitting the blond man if it missed its original target.

Wellard had started climbing. There was a steel ladder attached to the side of the observation car facing the depot and he had begun scrambling up it. Hawkins grabbed at the man's right ankle and secured a firm grip upon it. Then he received Wellard's left heel in his face by way of retaliation. An iron quarter tip split his nostrils and blood flew, but he hung on grimly, hauling himself onto the ladder in his enemy's wake and heaving himself up until his face was level with the backs of Wellard's knees.

A revolver banged, and Hawkins flinched as scalding lead splattered off a metal rung even with his forehead. It made him question whether his strategy had been so clever after all. Thomson and Dunbar were clearly not going to let his presence close to Wellard deter them from firing directly at him. A second detonation boomed at Hawkins' back. He winced, expecting to die; but, far short of that, he didn't even hear what became of the bullet. Wondering why not, he threw a glance down over his left shoulder and saw Ellen Copperstone sitting in the black grit below him and holding up a smoking gun — while the ponderous Frank Dunbar, standing opposite her, was clutching at his bulging midriff and trying to hold back the blood pouring out of a bullet-hole there. The hardcase sat down with a thump, then rolled onto a propping right elbow — plainly dying — and Les Thomson cursed and turned his Colt on the woman who had plugged his comrade; but she drilled him through the middle before he could pull the trigger and he went sailing backwards as if hit by a battering ram and finally spreadeagled.

The villain's death took a load off Hawkins' mind. Now it was one against one again. He went for Wellard's legs with renewed determination, trying to jerk Wellard off the steel ladder and pitch him to the ground below. But the fair-haired young man, with Hellenic build, was too strong for that and, short of being dislodged, actually reacted to Hawkins' increased efforts with a matching output of power; and he kicked himself out of his opponent's clutches and dazed Hawkins anew with another heel in the face. Going on unobstructed after that, he completed his ascent to the roof of the observation car. Here, with his feet gathered over the handrails at the top of the ladder, he went crabbing forward past the ventilators and soon reached the further end of the roof, where he came erect and now drew the revolver for which he had earlier reached inside his coat.

Hawkins arrived at the top of the metal ladder just then. He stood gazing along the roof of the car with his feet more or less rooted on the rungs beneath him. He found that he had neither the energy nor the wit left to do anything more than meet the eyes of the man beyond him. Wellard had been too much for him, and he sensed the other's amused contempt and wished to God that he still had a pistol in his grasp. But he was instead forced to watch the cruelty gathering in the blond man's eyes as Wellard cocked his weapon and took a deliberate aim, his finger curling about the trigger with a kind of avidity that also held a touch of madness.

It was all too easy for Wellard, and Hawkins felt suddenly enraged that life had let him down like this. He had come through so much only to die tamely at the end. But then, however, a swift movement began beneath him and, from the tail of his eyes, Hawkins saw Ellen Copperstone running into a position from which she could cover the blond figure rearing on top of the observation car. Wellard sensed her shift of position too and momentarily slanting his gaze to the right and down, called: "Don't you dare, Ellen!"

"You come down this instant, Jason!" the girl warned in her turn. "I'm not playing!"

"And you think I am?" Wellard jeered. "I'll kill you also if I have to!"

"Jason, you've done me harm enough," Ellen said soberly. "If there's any more killing to be done, it will be you who dies."

"Cut it out, Ellen, and go away!"

The girl went on standing there, her gun pointing upwards.

"Don't threaten me, Ellen!" Wellard snarled. "For the last time, will you — ?"

But Ellen was already slowly shaking

her head and her expression was implacable.

"Have it then!" Wellard bawled, angling his gun into line with his downward gaze and pulling the trigger.

He missed, but the girl didn't, and he clutched at himself and did a forward roll off the roof of the observation car, coming to rest at her feet and staring skywards with blank eyes that still registered disbelief.

Silently whistling his relief — for feelings of shame were one thing and death quite another — Hawkins climbed back down to the cinder track and walked the few steps necessary to reach the girl's side. "You sure got me out of that one!" he acknowledged. "You saved my life, and that makes my life yours, doesn't it?"

"You've been doing your best for me, Sam."

"I have," he agreed. "But talk about Sixgun Venus! Where in tarnation blazes did you learn to shoot like that?"

"There's no mystery in that," Ellen replied. "My late father used to say: 'If God gives you more then others, Satan will always force you to defend it. You'd better learn how to do it properly, Ellen'. So he had an Army marksman teach me how to shoot."

"That guy, whoever he was, sure earned his pay!" Hawkins commented with feeling, gently turning the girl about and walking her back to the spot where Wellard had dropped her jewel box, more or less unnoticed, at the beginning of the showdown. "I guess you'd better pick your trinkets up, lady."

"No, you pick them up," Ellen said. "I can't think of any man I'd rather have keep them safe for me — until our waggon train reaches Sacramento."

"Okay," he said. "But I'll God-damn see my neck as long as my arm before you're going on to that consarned Priceless Gulch. Hell-and-dammit, I won't lose you anyhow at all, not now, my woman!"

"Sam, you really must stop swearing like that!" Ellen chided. "How am I ever to make a gentleman of you?"

Now that was an interesting one, and it might have had Hawkins mightily worried, but he could see the girl was laughing to herself.

THE END

FIGHTING RAMROD
Charles N. Heckelmann

Most men would have cut their losses, but Frazer counted the bullets in his guns and said he'd soak the range in blood before he'd give up another inch of what was his.

LONE GUN
Eric Allen

Smoke Blackbird had been away too long. The Lequires had seized the Blackbird farm, forcing the Indians and settlers off, and no one seemed willing to fight! He had to fight alone.

THE THIRD RIDER
Barry Cord

Mel Rawlins wasn't going to let anything stand in his way. His father was murdered, his two brothers gone. Now Mel rode for vengeance.

ARIZONA DRIFTERS
W. C. Tuttle

When drifting Dutton and Lonnie Steelman decide to become partners they find that they have a common enemy in the formidable Thurston brothers.

TOMBSTONE
Matt Braun

Wells Fargo paid Luke Starbuck to outgun the silver-thieving stagecoach gang at Tombstone. Before long Luke can see the only thing bearing fruit in this eldorado will be the gallows tree.

HIGH BORDER RIDERS
Lee Floren

Buckshot McKee and Tortilla Joe cut the trail of a border tough who was running Mexican beef into Texas. They stopped the smuggler in his tracks.

BRETT RANDALL, GAMBLER
E. B. Mann

Larry Day had the choice of running away from the law or of assuming a dead man's place. No matter what he decided he was bound to end up dead.

THE GUNSHARP
William R. Cox

The Eggerleys weren't very smart. They trained their sights on Will Carney and Arizona's biggest blood bath began.

THE DEPUTY OF SAN RIANO
Lawrence A. Keating and
Al. P. Nelson

When a man fell dead from his horse, Ed Grant was spotted riding away from the scene. The deputy sheriff rode out after him and came up against everything from gunfire to dynamite.

FARGO: MASSACRE RIVER
John Benteen

The ambushers up ahead had now blocked the road. Fargo's convoy was a jumble, a perfect target for the insurgents' weapons!

SUNDANCE: DEATH IN THE LAVA
John Benteen

The Modoc's captured the wagon train and its cargo of gold. But now the halfbreed they called Sundance was going after it . . .

HARSH RECKONING
Phil Ketchum

Five years of keeping himself alive in a brutal prison had made Brand tough and careless about who he gunned down . . .

FARGO: PANAMA GOLD
John Benteen

With foreign money behind him, Buckner was going to destroy the Panama Canal before it could be completed. Fargo's job was to stop Buckner.

FARGO:
THE SHARPSHOOTERS
John Benteen

The Canfield clan, thirty strong were raising hell in Texas. Fargo was tough enough to hold his own against the whole clan.

PISTOL LAW
Paul Evan Lehman

Lance Jones came back to Mustang for just one thing — revenge! Revenge on the people who had him thrown in jail.

HELL RIDERS
Steve Mensing

Wade Walker's kid brother, Duane, was locked up in the Silver City jail facing a rope at dawn. Wade was a ruthless outlaw, but he was smart, and he had vowed to have his brother out of jail before morning!

DESERT OF THE DAMNED
Nelson Nye

The law was after him for the murder of a marshal — a murder he didn't commit. Breen was after him for revenge — and Breen wouldn't stop at anything . . . blackmail, a frameup . . . or murder.

DAY OF THE COMANCHEROS
Steven C. Lawrence

Their very name struck terror into men's hearts — the Comancheros, a savage army of cutthroats who swept across Texas, leaving behind a bloodstained trail of robbery and murder.

SUNDANCE: SILENT ENEMY
John Benteen

A lone crazed Cheyenne was on a personal war path. They needed to pit one man against one crazed Indian. That man was Sundance.

LASSITER
Jack Slade

Lassiter wasn't the kind of man to listen to reason. Cross him once and he'll hold a grudge for years to come — if he let you live that long.

LAST STAGE TO GOMORRAH
Barry Cord

Jeff Carter, tough ex-riverboat gambler, now had himself a horse ranch that kept him free from gunfights and card games. Until Sturvesant of Wells Fargo showed up.